The Little Girl From Yesterday

Vika Winters

THE LITTLE GIRL FROM YESTERDAY

This book is a work of fiction. Names, characters, places and events are entirely fictitious or used in a fictitious manner. This story is a product of the author's imagination.

www.vikawinters.com
www.simplyv.blogspot.com (English)
www.lvjp.blogspot.com (Portuguese)
vikawinters@gmail.com

3rd edition

To my BFFs, Beta and Lua.

To my hubby, Dean, who puts up with me.

And to my four moms –
Iacy de Souza,
Iara Suely,
Léa Sylvia,
and Inajá Cleide –
who all claim ownership over me.

Contents

1 *The Little Boy From Yesterday*

The display on the dashboard filled with colorful buttons and blinking lights was showing the number 1986. Vítor opened the hatch of what looked like a spaceship and peeked outside. Nothing had changed except for the cars in the parking lot. He stepped out of the ship onto the play area of the condo complex where he lived with his parents.

Still a bit dizzy holding on to his machine, he was able to see his mom walking through the gate. She was holding the hand of a six-year-old boy in a school uniform, who carried a tiny backpack on his shoulders. In her other hand, Mom held a rose and a heart-shaped card, a special gift the school had prepared for Mother's Day.

Vítor ran up to her and asked, "Can you tell me what time it is now?"

"Twenty past twelve," she replied with a smile.

Vítor looked at his watch and noticed that it was ten minutes behind. He called out to his mother, who was already going up the stairs, "Hey! Happy Mother's Day!"

She thanked him without looking back. The boy, with a victorious smile, ran back to his machine and closed the hatch.

*

That same afternoon, over the phone, he retold the morning event.

"Six years old! Can you believe that? I was right there, standing in front of myself, at six years old!"

"No, I don't believe it," Vicky said in the midst of giggles.

7

"Well, you'd better believe it. It really did work."

"Vítor, are you serious? You've traveled seven years back in time?"

"Vicky, I was never this serious."

They were silent for a few seconds, and Vítor went on, "So... do you believe me?"

"I only believe what I can see," Vicky said.

"So you're in?" he asked.

"Of course! You know I'm crazy anyway. And besides, it's the Beatles we're talking about, old man. If it's about the Beatles, I'm in. I was born in."

"I knew it. So why don't you come over this weekend?"

"Sounds great. Tonight I will ask my mom to call yours, and they can set us up for the weekend."

"Okay, but don't forget, she can only call after nine."

No reply. Vicky had dived into a sea of dreams.

"You hear me?"

"Yeah... after nine," she replied, still involved in her own thoughts.

"So... we will tell them that you're spending the weekend, okay?"

"Okay, yeah, we'll say I am going to study with you... for the finals."

"Oh, and obviously, *you* are going to teach *me* English."

"Of course, old man. I am the good student here."

They laughed. They knew that wasn't the whole truth. Both friends had their weaknesses and strengths. And because they both had parents who held them to fairly high standards, they'd learned to help each other out in order to keep all of their grades high. Well, at least as high as they could. But Vicky liked to brag.

Vítor, however, did not let her get away with it. "Yeah, think what you want, dude. Try passing math without me."

"Oh, how dare you!"

Vicky slammed the phone as she used to do whenever he aggravated her. But she had a smile on her face. She was sitting on her mom's bed holding a jokes book she had just bought on the way home from school. She always had a new jokes book in hand. On the bed, there were some schoolbooks and some notebooks covered with Beatles and Paul McCartney pictures. Homework had long been done and the TV was on, showing the Afternoon Session.

The Afternoon Session is a weekday movie hour on Globo TV[1] that features any movie that's too old for prime-time TV, regardless of rating. That's how most Brazilian city kids, like Vicky, get to watch Freddy Krueger and Jason Voorhees movies.

1Globo TV is Brazil's cultural glue. They dictate cultural trends such as clothing and vocabulary.

After all, any Brazilian city child knows that playing outside is just too dangerous! It is so much safer to watch horror and violent movies on TV.

On that day, however, all that was on was the harmless 1987 movie *Can't Buy Me Love*, a comic movie featuring a Beatles song. Vicky had seen the commercial the day before, and she knew she had to see that movie. But suddenly a movie featuring a Beatles song just sounded lame. *Who needs that? I'll soon have the real deal.* She glanced at her math notebook, which was covered exclusively with pictures of Paul McCartney, and wondered, *Could it be?*

Well, could it be? The Beatles, the most famous band in the history of mankind, broke up ten years before Vicky was born. John Lennon, the Beatles' mastermind, was killed the year she was born. She became a Beatles fan at age ten when she was watching a John Lennon tribute on Globo TV. And Paul McCartney, her favorite one, now had a wife, children, and a successful solo career of his own. Vicky would never be able see the Beatles play live. And she would never be able to be Paul's girl. Not under normal circumstances. But now things were anything but normal.

2 Travel Time!

By late afternoon on the following Friday, Mom drove Vicky to spend the weekend at her friend Vítor's place. When they got there, they found him at the playground. He was wearing his blue jersey from basketball school, and his long brownish hair shone in the sun. His face, as always, was a constant reminder of the man of her dreams, Paul McCartney. But she didn't say that out loud anymore. Not to Vítor.

The girl bid her mom farewell, walked through the gate, and waved good-bye until she saw the car disappear down the hill.

"*Sup*, Vitty! Give me five!" she said as her hand went up to greet the boy.

He returned the high five. "Hey, Vicky. What's up?"

"The sky, old man."

"Are you ready?" he asked with a fun smile.

"Can't think of anything else." She also smiled. "Where is it?"

"Come with me."

They walked together toward the side of the building. Vítor pulled a long white sheet that was covering the huge machine and introduced it, "Ehem! Ehem! Ladies and gentlemen! It is my pleasure to introduce to you, unheard of in human history, the time machine! Magic Vítor!"

Vicky chuckled. "You named your machine Magic Vítor."

"Yeah. So?"

"Like, Magic Johnson?"

"Ah, give me a break, Vicky. I like the dude, okay. I will be like him someday."

"Vítor, you're Brazilian. You're supposed to like soccer, not basketball."

Vítor paid no attention to her remarks and went on, "So? Ready?"

The girl hesitated. "Hmm... er... Vítor, do you think that'll really work?"

"Of course. Are you doubting me? Doubting my astuteness?"

"Oh, you silly. Don't start with the crazy words."

"Why not? You do it all the time," he teased.

"Vítor, my darling, do you want a punch in the middle of your beautiful nose?" she asked, hitting her right fist against her left hand.

Vítor was not really scared of her. He was really scared of the idea that if a girl hits you, you're not supposed to hit back. *A coward is a man who hits a woman.*

"Calm down! Look, chill, okay! Everything will be just fine. Trust me. Did you bring everything you'll need?"

"I sure did. I've checked more than a million times."

"Sure. How long did it take you to pack?" he asked cynically.

"Shut up, freak."

Vítor laughed and went on to a quick explanation of how the machine was supposed to work. Then he asked, "Which day do you want to go to? Any idea?"

"Well, I was looking at my Beatles book, and... it can be anywhere between March twentieth and May thirty-first of nineteen sixty-four. It seems like there were no major trips or events happening in those days."

Vítor watched her with a pensive look for a moment. He hopped on the machine, typed something that made the screen display the calendar of 1964, and said, "April thirtieth, nineteen sixty-four. It's a Thursday" He then turned to Vicky. "Is that good?"

"So... when do I get back?"

"Saturday, May second, in the evening. You have two days to do whatever you want. And you'll be back just in time for your mom to pick you up."

"Perfect."

Vítor typed in a few more keys, hopped off the machine, and said, "So get in and buckle up."

Vicky hesitated again. "Better watch what you're about to do to me, hey, you cuckoo."

"B-b-but, Vicky, isn't meeting the Beatles your greatest dream ever? Are you chickening out?"

No, she wasn't chickening out. It was just that, at that exact moment, her feelings were going on a roller coaster ride. Actually, she felt exactly as you would feel if you had just decided to get in the line for the front cart of the highest roller coaster on Earth. As much as you'd know it would be the best ride of your life, you'd keep second-guessing yourself.

"Chill, dude. It's all controlled by the machine. See, here is how it works. There are two settings. Look," he pointed to the dashboard. "Setting one, the machine goes with you, so you're in charge of bringing yourself back. You don't want to do that. Too complicated. Setting two, the machine sends you there and brings you back on a preset time. It will find you, and it will bring you back. You don't have to worry about a thing. It is safer than riding the Lacerda elevator."

Vítor was referring to the highest and most famous outdoor elevator in the world, which happened to be in the city where they lived – Salvador, Bahia.

"Are you sure it is *really* safe?"

"No doubt about it. Just trust me on this, okay. Oh, I can't forget to tell this, you just have to follow two basic safety rules."

"Which are?"

"First, you can go anywhere you want, but do not leave town when it's time to come back. Or else the machine won't be able to locate you to bring you back. And even more important, whatever happens, don't tell anyone anything. Remember how dangerous it can be to alter the continuum. Not a peep. Is that cool?"

So if she left Liverpool at the right time, she thought, he would not be able to bring her back. So if things really worked out... that would be easy to arrange. Vicky was already making plans. Vítor, however, was still waiting for her answer.

"Is that cool?" he asked again

"Oh… yeah… Yeah, that's cool."

"Now, remember, your return is programmed for two days from now. Two days, got it? Do anything, go anywhere you want, but be in Liverpool in *two days*!"

"Okay."

"Okay. God be with you, and good luck."

"If anything bad happens to me…" she threatened and did her fist-punching-hand thing.

Vítor shook his head. "Oh, Vicky!"

"Calm down! I'm in here."

"Fine. Well, now it is five fifty. You'll get there at exactly nine p.m. their time."

"Why so late?"

"Because the machine has a ten-minute lag from departure to arrival, even though we only feel as if a minute has passed.

Besides, there is the three-hour difference of the time zone."

"Oh… Ok, whatever. Bye."

Vicky anxiously closed the hatch before she changed her mind again.

He warned, "Attention for the countdown: five... four..."
"Dude. Really?"
"... three... two... one... go!"
He then turned a key, pushed a button, and the machine began to spin.

3 A Two-Day Deal

~~~~ 1993 ~~~~1990 ~~~~1984 ~~~~1980~~~~
~~~~1974 ~~~~1970 ~~~~1964 ~~~~

In 1964, at nine o'clock at night, dizzy due to the machine rotation, and trying to keep her balance, Vicky found herself in Liverpool, England, right in front of Paul McCartney's home, which looked exactly like the one she had seen in the Beatles' movie *Help!*

She ran to the door and rang the bell. At this point, her heart was at a million beats per second. *Is this for real?* she thought.

But something was wrong. She looked down and grabbed the door frame, trying to keep herself up. The machine was gone, but the world was still spinning. Fast.

I don't feel good.

*

Inside the house, the four Beatles were playing "Thank You Girl" when they heard the bell. Paul got up, walked to the door, and looked through the peephole.

"Who is it, Paul?" John asked.

"It's just a little girl."

"But at this time," John said to the others.

Paul opened the door. "Hi. What's up?"

Vicky was still looking down when she heard the door moving. Now her eyes were wide-open, fixed on the guy that had just opened the door and talked to her. *Come on! Say something! And yes, it's him!*

"I, I-uh…"

Well, that did it. The emotion of being in front of the one person she'd always dreamed of meeting, plus the dizziness from the trip was all it took. She'd never thought she'd ever faint. But she did – luckily, in Paul's arms.

"Oh, nice," he said, and pulled her inside. "Hey, John, a little help here."

"What's up?"

"The girl fainted."

"Oh, big news," John remarked, walking toward Paul without any rush.

Ringo and George just watched.

"I will just lay her on the couch."

"You might want to take her backpack off her back," Ringo said while walking their way.

"Probably a good idea."

Then George remembered, "I'll go get some ammonia."

"Brilliant. *That* will wake her up," John said.

Paul sat by Vicky's side while John and Ringo remained standing. George soon came back with a bottle of ammonia.

"Here you are," he said as he brought the bottle up close to her face.

Vicky came to, frightened, and the first thing she saw was Paul's cute face. Well, that was quite a startle. She almost could not believe it.

"P-P-Paul? Paul McCartney? Is that really you? I mean, I mean, you guys are… the Beatles?"

"Are-eh. Yeah," he said, chuckling at the girl's amazement.

She sat up on the couch. "You're George Harrison, right? And you're Ringo Starr! And you are… John Lennon! I… I can't believe it! Guys! The Beatles!"

"Oh, you can believe it," Ringo joked, "'cause that's us."

"Hmm…but… What happened? Why am I sitting here?"

John explained as if it were the most common thing in the world. "You fainted, so Paul brought you inside."

"I? Fainted? And in Paul McCartney's arms? Old man! I can't believe it!"

"So do you ever believe anything?" Paul joked. "But, okay, you knocked on my door. What was it that you wanted?"

"Me? Well, I... Why, I just wanted to hang out with you guys. Old man! If I tell that to my school gang, no one will ever believe me." Vicky took a few seconds to look around. "Wow! This house is just like the one in the movie! And they say you can't believe the stuff you see on TV." She hurried to check out

19

John Lennon's bed. According to the movie, his bed was in a hole in the floor, which she thought to be an incredibly funny idea. And there it was! "Do you really sleep in here, old man?"

That was when she noticed how the young men looked at each other confused. What did she mean by hang out?

"Well, you see, I come from a very, very faraway land. The thing is, my greatest dream ever was to meet you guys. So my friend Vítor—my best friend ever—found a way to bring me here. So I came, obviously. I would not pass on that chance. Oh, by the way, my name is Vitória."

"Victoria?" George asked, confused.

"No. Vitória. It's like Victoria, but in my language. It's Regina Vitória. But I go by Vicky."

"Vicky,"John said, "I see you brought your backpack."

"Yup."

"And … why? You're not intending to stay here, right? I mean, at Paul's place."

"But of course I am! Listen to yourself! Where on earth could I possibly stay?"

"I don't know. With your folks?"

"Don't you get it? I'm here by myself. The only person that knows about it is Vítor. He brought me here. And he is the only one who can take me back. In two days. So … like … I'm kind of here for the weekend."

The boys stood silent at the sound of that.

Vicky kept glancing at Paul, hoping he'd say something. Her heart was racing again. He, on the other hand, just watched her, trying to figure out what on earth was going on. *Quite a nerve this little girl has*, he thought.

However, while Ringo and George sent worried looks to Paul, John asked, "What if we say you can't stay?"

"*Oxe*![2] And you're going to throw me out in the streets? I can't go back without Vítor's help."

"Can't go back? Well, I don't know how you got here, but we

---

2 Oxe is a regional interjection. People in Bahia, the state Vicky was born and raised in, say *oxe* almost as often as they breathe.

can always find a flight back to your country."

"No! N-n-n-no! You can't!"

"And why not?"

"Well… It is that…the place I live is really far away. Right. That's it. There are no flights there because no one has ever heard of it."

"What do you mean?" George intervened. "There is no place on Earth that no one knows."

"Trust me on this one, old man. This place I come from is really unknown. Seriously."

No one got that nonsense. Ringo looked jokingly at Vicky and asked, "Where on earth do you come from? Another planet?"

"*Oxe*! Of course not! *E.T.* is Spielberg's stuff."

Well, she really lost everyone then because Spielberg's *E.T.* would not come around for another sixteen years. Globo TV had been showing it every year around Christmastime for as long as Vicky had been alive. She could not conceive a world in which *E.T.* did not exist and in which Spielberg was not a synonym for adventure, technology, and great movies. But, to any British kid in the sixties, neither *E.T.* nor Spielberg meant anything at all.

Vicky was still glancing at Paul and thinking, *Please, say something, like "Sure, you can hang out with us. And by the way, I think I'm in love with you."* It could just be that easy, couldn't it?

He did decide to say something. He was trying to figure her out, so he looked right into her eyes and pleaded, "Come on, just tell us these two things. Where do you come from? And why can you only go back home with your friend's help in two days?"

Paul's sweet smile and tilted eyes that, until that day, Vicky had only seen in pictures made her want to tell everything. But she was not supposed to. So she risked this suggestion. "Look, Vítor told me I should not, under any circumstance, say anything to anyone. But for you, Paul, I'd be willing to compromise. So I want to make a deal with you."

"What deal?"

"Let me stay here … for these two days … with you … and no questions about this matter. Then, before I leave, I'll tell you everything. I promise. And I promise you'll like what you'll hear. All right?"

John did not buy that. "How can we know that you're not tricking us? Then you'll tell the whole world that you spent two days at Paul's home. Easy, eh."

George agreed. "That's right. How do we know you're telling the truth?"

But Paul didn't think the same way. It sounded crazy, but he did not think she was lying. "Hey, mates, wait. I think she's telling the truth." Then to Vicky, he said, "I still think you're talking crazy, but I don't think you're lying." He looked back to his friends. "What is it going to cost us if we trust her? Right?"

"I don't know… This is just too odd." John was still not buying it.

"Oh, come on. Look at her. Why would she want to trick us?"

"Does free stay at Paul McCartney's house ring a bell, mate?"

Well, Paul had no answer for that. He shrugged and quickly glanced at his three friends then back at Vicky, who stared at him, not knowing what to do.

She should have planned a convincing cover story. Now she was at the mercy of probably the most famous guys in the whole world, and they had no idea who she was, and there was no reason why she should be allowed to hang out with them.

There was silence for a moment. Then George turned to John. "If she is really telling the truth, only she and this bloke Vítor know she's here. Isn't it kind of funny that a kid travels halfway around the world and no grownups know about it?"

"You're right." And he turned to Vicky. "Then what about your parents? You have parents, right?"

"Duh. I mean, only my mom. She dropped me off at Vítor's house for the weekend. And his parents work all day long. They think we're studying. So? Can you at least agree with the deal and try to be my friends for a change? Two days."

"What do you think, mates?" John asked.

Paul jumped right in. "You know what I think."

Ringo, who'd been friendly from the beginning, agreed.

George just shook his shoulders.

Then John shrugged and said that if that was what everyone else thought, then fine, she could stay. "And, anyway, Paul, it's your house."

The girl celebrated. "Cool! Cool! You guys are the best!"

"But then, so what? Since you're stuck here for two days, what do you think you want to do with all that time?"

"I...uh..."

John, George, Ringo, and Paul watched her, waiting for a reply. Vicky had heard the question but had not really listened to it. She just stood there because what she was really doing was gazing at Paul's face. Finally she said, "Oh my, I was right!"

Trying to sound natural, he asked, "Are you okay, girl?"

"Uh, yeah. I just... Did you know you look exactly like Vítor?"

"Oh yeah?"

"Of course. You're Vítor spitting and sneezing."

Everyone laughed at the weird Brazilian phrase the girl used. But she did not realize that and went on. "The only difference is your hair. Vítor's hair is brownish and long. Like, this long," she said, putting her hands halfway down her back to give the guys an idea of the length of her friend's hair.

John tried to understand. "Is this Vítor a bloke? Or a gal?"

"*Oxe*! Of course he's a boy!"

Oxe was another word that made them look at each other and sneer every time she said it. Who'd ever heard that before? No one in England at least. The guys didn't know where she was from, but they just thought that the word sounded funny and assumed she said funny words because she was not a local.

"And where you live, is it common for boys to wear hair that long?" asked John.

"Most common thing in the world. Your hair is short compared to over there."

"So odd," John replied.

23

"Yeah, everything is different from here. Totally different."

"Intriguing. I want to know more about this place of yours," Paul wished.

"Don't worry, Paul. One day you will know all about it. For real. You know, we have video games, *Jurassic Park*, you'll like it. It's da beast![3]"

"It's da what? What do you mean?"

"Hmm, well"—she smiled, trying to sound mysterious—"you'll find out."

One more time, the four of them looked at each other, not able to figure things out.

So Ringo figured, "Oh! Are you from one of those socialist countries that we don't know anything about?"

"*Oxe*! You crazy? Thank God I am not. No way. To tell the truth, I don't care much for socialism. But I know a joke about Russians. Do you guys like jokes?"

"I do."

"Old man, I have a whole inventory of jokes."

"Brilliant. What do you have?"

"Listen to this one. They say there was a Russian army standing in six long lines. So when the captain was walking by the first line…"

The Russian army joke got lost in translation, so it did not impress anyone, but Vicky made them all crack up with the story of the Japanese guy that gets stuck in the bathroom and the story of the two babies in the maternity room. Then she tried to convince everyone that people really have eleven fingers and made a fool out of Paul with the straight-hand test. Telling jokes and playing pranks was Vicky's way of getting grownups to open up. It always worked. Apparently, it was working again. She was getting to please everyone and convince them she really meant no harm.

Eventually, she asked, "But what were you guys doing?"

"We? Oh, you mean before you arrived? We were playing

---

3 It's da beast! (*É o bicho!*) Nineties slang in Bahia. "It's awesome!"

some songs," Paul replied.

"Well, well, well. Who am I to stay in the way?" she said with a smile. "Please, play a little bit more."

You bet that's what she wanted. She had only traveled thirty years in the past. And this way, she got to hear a little bit more of "Thank You Girl" and a few other songs live at Paul's home. Who would ever believe that back at home?

4 *Professor Gilmar*

Now here's the problem with both Vítor and Vicky: they were braggers. Both of them knew very well that the time machine experience was supposed to be kept secret, but they talked about it everywhere they went, including school, and did not always care to make sure no one else was listening in.

Due to this negligence of the two friends, a boy from school named Edu overheard them more than once. Then he asked Vítor a few nonchalant questions, and got the information he wanted.

Everyone in school knew Edu had a problem with both Vicky and Vítor. Since Vicky had always found good grace with the teachers, Edu thought hanging out with her would get him some points in school. But would you date a brownnose? Neither would she. The problem was that he wasn't about to leave it alone.

While Vicky and Vítor were getting ready to time travel, Edu had scheduled to meet Professor Gilmar at the bus stop down the hill from Vítor's home.

Professor Gilmar was the teacher Vicky and her gang loved to annoy. Probably the most hated teacher in the whole Ruy Barbosa Institute[4]. It was not like he did not deserve it. The guy had secrets that went beyond the realm of honesty. He was no longer working at the Institute because everyone had already found out about his issues. Edu, however, didn't care about that

---

4Their school was named after Ruy Barbosa - a writer, jurist, politician and diplomat born in Salvador, Bahia. Also known as the Eagle of Hague for his notorious participation in the 2nd Hague Peace Convention (in the Netherlands).

at all. He wanted to mess with Vítor and Vicky, and so he yapped away.

"But what are you saying, Eduardo? Is that some kind of joke?"

"Joke? Do you want to go see and believe it?"

"But where?"

"Right up this hill. Come with me."

If Edu was right, that was the chance Gilmar had been hoping for to get even with Vicky. Besides, if a time machine was real, the possibilities were never-ending. So he followed Edu. The two of them went up the hill that led to the ground floor of Vítor's condo complex. And there he was, looking serious and proud, standing next to his machine.

From the gate, Edu called out, "Hey, Vítor!"

Vítor did not like what he saw, but out of sheer good manners, he said, "Sup, Edu! Come on in."

Edu went in and asked if Vítor remembered Professor Gilmar from last year. Of course he did. How couldn't he?

Vítor wanted to twist Edu's neck when he found out the teacher had come over to see *his* machine. But Edu was not about to hang around and wait for his execution. He said good-bye and left, leaving Professor Gilmar alone with Vítor. When Vítor noticed that Edu was going down the hill laughing his pants off, his blood started to boil.

"Vítor, does that really work? I mean, is it real?"

An inconsequential excitement immediately replaced Vítor's anger. "Of course! I just sent Vicky to nineteen sixty-four!" Right away, he regretted saying that. Couldn't he have denied it? Said it was all just a big joke? But no. He let himself be driven by pride, and that was it. His big mouth told everything.

"So how does it work?"

This time the teacher's strategy didn't work.

"Do you think I look stupid, dude? Do you think I will tell you that?" Vítor shook his head. "Do me a favor, nonresidents are not allowed in the play area. So get out of here. Please."

"What's up, Vítor? What is the problem in you explaining me

how this works? If it really works," he teased.

"Oh, of course it works." Vítor replied, offended.

"So prove it. Send me where you sent your friend."

"No."

"Why not?"

"For two reasons. First, the machine is tracking the place and the date where Vicky is right now, and it's working on the countdown to bring her back. It can't be used before she gets back or else that's it. We lose contact, everything gets out of place, and kaboom! She doesn't come back, you don't come back, no one comes back. Second, what sort of a retard do you take me for? A mongoloid like Edu? I know you don't like Vicky, and I know why. Actually, I'm surprised you're being nice to me. But I would have to be an idiot to send you to ruin her life. Now, get out, please."

Gilmar acted as if he had lost that battle. He turned around, pretending he was leaving, but unexpectedly, he turned back to the boy, now with a cheap pocketknife in his hand. He grabbed Vítor by the shirt and pushed him against a pillar.

"Listen, boy, you guys have already done way too much damage to my life! You tell me how the machine works if you like your head where it is!"

"Hey, dude! Chill!" Vítor begged, frightened by the unexpected attitude of the teacher.

"Come on, boy! How do I use the machine?" he yelled.

Seeing no way out, Vítor pointed to the machine and revealed, "Inside it there's an on/off button. You just have to push it and follow the directions that come up in the screen. It's like an ATM - with options, everything."

"Thanks, idiot."

He grabbed the boy by the hair and hit his head against the pillar, leaving him unconscious. After that, he ran to the machine and followed Vítor's explanation.

5 *A Very Odd Phone Call*

~~~ 1993 ~~~1990 ~~~~1984 ~~~~1980~~~
~~~~1974 ~~~~1970 ~~~ 1964 ~~~

It was 9:10 p.m. Gilmar looked around, still dizzy, and with a smile, he said to himself, "Incredible! Liverpool, England, 1964. Well, now let's take care of a few things."

*

A little while later at Paul's house, Vicky and her new friends were eating a late-night snack and listening to music.

"So, Paul, I don't know anything about England. Do you think it would be cool to go out tomorrow? Like sightseeing?"

"Well I am not sure what you know about the Beatles in your country, but…it's kind of hard for us to go anywhere around here without drawing quite a crowd."

"Yeah, I know. I've seen documentaries about you."

"Documentaries? About us? What are you talking about?"

"Did I say documentaries? I meant news stories. I get confused with words sometimes. I don't speak your language very well."

"You don't? But … you don't … have an accent."

"I don't? You mean it?"

"Yeah. I'm not trying to be nice. You really don't."

Hmm, that was interesting. She didn't have an accent? But she'd never learned to speak British English. As a matter of fact, she didn't even speak American English that well. She had been learning English for only two years. Actually, she hadn't thought

31

about that before. How was it that it was suddenly so easy to talk to the Beatles? Vítor! He'd done something! But she didn't want to think about Vítor then. She wanted to think about what she could do with the Beatles. So she ignored the accent issue. "But... So you never go anywhere? Like, do you ever go to the movies?"

"It's quite a project," John explained. "It's quite a project doing anything that's normal and easy for a gal like you."

"Hey, I'm famous too, you know."

"Oh really?"

"Really. In my school."

"Oh yeah, of course. Same thing. You can relate to our lives," he said.

"I'm serious. Everybody knows me. Everybody likes me. 'Cause I can give people the answers to the exams in my classroom and in other classrooms ... at the same time! Now ask me how I do that. Not telling ya!"

"So yer famous for helpin' people cheat."

"I'm famous for *helping* people. But see? I'm just as famous as you are. I can relate."

"Sure you can," Ringo joked.

"So are we, like, stuck in the house?"

Paul suggested, "Why don't we just go for a drive tonight? Unless it's bedtime for you."

"Bedtime? You kidding me? D'you see my mom anywhere here? No, no. I could stay up all night with you guys."

"Brilliant. So let's go for a drive? You can get to know our city."

"But at night?"

"Why not?"

"*Oxe*! You cannot see anything!"

"Yes, you can. Don't you have streetlights in your country?"

"You suggesting that I come from an uncivilized world?"

"I'm not suggesting anything. You said it."

"So can we go see, like, Big Ben?"

Everyone laughed.

"That's in London! It's three hours away!" Paul clarified.

"Oh."

"You really don't know much about this country, do you?"

"No, I don't," she admitted. "But I know a lot about you. I read everything I find about you. My teachers say that's a good thing. That you're supposed to find something you're passionate about and read, read, *read*. That's how you learn to think, you know. By reading."

Paul nodded, thinking that was funny. "I guess ... I'm glad to be of service to your education? Now, okay, little girl, Liverpool is all you get for tonight. Do you want to do that at all?"

"Sure. But first, can I go shower and—" And, out of the blue, Vicky gasped. Her tone of voice suddenly changed to that of someone who just had the most amazing idea in the world. "Guys, do you still play at the Cavern Club? Can we go there?"

"The Cavern?" John repeated her words.

The four of them smiled as friends who recall good old times. The Cavern Club was this little, tiny club in Liverpool where the Beatles used to play before they were super famous all over the world.

And John himself explained, "No, we don't play there anymore. But nothing stops us from going there tonight."

"Yeah, yeah, yeah! Let's do it! Let's do it!"

"And, hey," Paul remembered, "tomorrow afternoon we are going to the BBC in London. You're welcome to come. And then you can probably catch a glimpse of Big Ben."

"Of course I will."

"Now, Vicky, you don't really have to shower. It's kind of getting late and—"

"Oh no! Of course I do! I gotta look nice to hang out with you."

"But you look just fine the way you are now."

"No, I don't!" That said, she grabbed her backpack, walked into the bathroom, and slammed and locked the door, leaving Paul to shake his head and look at his pals.

But before anyone could say anything else, the door opened.

Vicky had a shy smile on her face. "Did you really just say I look fine?"

Paul sighed without much patience left. "Just go shower, Vicky."

"Okay, okay. No one has patience with me."

And the door closed again.

John, at this point, had a smirk on his face.

"Yeah," he kidded, "you look fine just the way you are, my love."

Paul looked at him, startled. "What? Shut up!"

When the bathroom door opened again some twenty minutes later, Vicky, already dressed up but still with a towel wrapped around her hair, looked beside herself with excitement. "I just had this *awesome* idea!"

"What's that?" Paul asked.

"Well, can't we go to Abbey Road?"

"Abbey Road?"

"Yeah, it's in London, right?"

"Uh…yes, that's where we record our albums. But why would you ever want to go there?"

"Uh, well, you said you tend to draw quite a crowd. But think. No one will be there."

"True, but—"

"I want to take a picture crossing the road!"

"A picture? Crossing Abbey Road?"

"Yeah, is that okay?"

"Uh… uh… I guess…"

"Sweet, dude!"

"Listen, are you done? Because—"

"Nope. Finishing up my hair."

She slammed the door again.

Paul looked at the others and asked, "What the heck was that loony talk all about?"

"What an odd idea," Ringo remarked.

"A picture crossing Abbey Road? I kind of like that idea," John replied with a smile. "I'm beginning to like this bird."

John didn't know that yet, but just few years in the future, he would use Vicky's idea and turn it into an album cover. And they'd call it (what do you know!) *Abbey Road*.

Then George, who had been quiet until that moment, whispered to Paul, "Are you sure that bringing her with us to the BBC is a good idea, mate?"

"What do you mean?"

"I mean, she's a child. And she does not look British at all. What if she's in the country illegally? Or what if her parents are looking for her? If her story is true, her family has no idea where she is. We already got in trouble when we traveled to Hamburg when I was underage, remember? You know what I mean?"

"Cheers, Georgie. That's probably what Brian would say," John added.

Vicky stuck her head out the door and said in a very excited voice, "You're talking about Brian Epstein, right? I know who he was. He was your manager. I've read about him. And about George Martin too. The fifth Beatle. They were the dudes who made sure everything happened in the background so you guys could focus on your music."

"Yes…right," John replied with a puzzled look on his face, not sure whether to worry about the fact that she was talking about them in the past tense or about the fact she'd been eavesdropping. "Shouldn't you be getting ready to go out instead of eavesdropping on grownups' talk?"

"I'm not eavesdropping! I'm just … I heard by chanc—well, let me finish getting ready."

As the door closed again, John said, "She's odd."

"What? You're still not used to girls trying to eavesdrop on you?" Ringo asked with a sarcastic smile.

As for Paul, he went on to reply to George's comment about Vicky's possible trouble, this time in a whisper, "Yeah, I'll see. I'll talk to her about London."

"He'll talk to her," John joked again.

"What's your game, mate?" Paul snapped at him.

"Forget it, Paul."

"She's a child, John!"

"Forget it, Paul!" John and George said together.

"Am I the only one here who thinks you're being sick?" Paul really wished John's jokes were over.

But John could see something that Paul couldn't in the girl's behavior. And he wasn't about to stop the jokes.

"All right." Vicky said, leaving bathroom. "Everyone ready?"

"Oh, finally," Paul said, getting up. "Let's go before the sun rises."

But the words had barely left his mouth when the phone rang. He hesitated for a second but decided to answer it.

"Hello."

"Mr. McCartney?"

"Who is this?"

"This is Interpol Agent McKenzie."

"Interpol?"

"Yes, and I am looking for a girl, uh, Vicky."

"What? Vicky?"

Everyone else immediately directed inquisitive looks at him.

"Isn't that what I just said?" the agent confirmed, sounding upset. Then he calmed himself down a little and went on. "I have informants who told me she was seen walking into your house. She's got slightly tanned skin and long curly black hair. Is it possible you have her with you?"

"Uh, ..."

The pause was so long that made Agent McKenzie prompt, "Well, do you have her or not?"

"Well, yeah, uh ... yeah, I- I guess we do have her with us, but—"

"Great. This is what you'll do: write down the address I will give you and take the girl there tonight at eleven-thirty. I will be there waiting for you. But you must go alone!"

Paul was not sure what to do. He looked at his friends, almost begging for help, but still, he grabbed a pen and paper and agreed. "Okay, go ahead."

Agent McKenzie gave Paul the address, and he wrote it

down. But not so sure about the whole situation, he still asked, "Can you tell me what this is about? Is it something serious, or did she just…run away from home?"

The agent was upset by that question. "That is none of your business! She's wanted by the Interpol, not by you!"

"What?" But Paul chose to keep his cool and just said, "Okay. Thank you anyway."

He hung up the phone without another word and buried his hands in his hair. His doubt of whether or not to believe what he had just heard brought a heavy silence into the house.

Everyone else anxiously waited for the report on the phone conversation. They all heard loudly and clearly when he said the words *Interpol* and *Vicky*. Something freaky was up.

John asked, "What is the matter, Paul?"

"Yeah, you were talking about me. To whom?"

Paul lifted up his head and looked into the girl's eyes. One could see he was sad, but trying not to be rude, he asked, "Why did you not tell me, Vicky?"

"Who? Me? Tell you? What?"

"But what is the matter, Paul?" John insisted.

Paul was indecisive, but at last, he said staring at the girl, "So the Interpol is coming for you."

"What? M-m-me?"

That was when the plot thickened. Vicky was not expecting anything like that and had not the least idea on how to deal with it.

As Paul heard her whining, he shook his head and looked down again.

John, Ringo, and George stared at her with surprised and nervous looks. She stared back at them with eyes that were no less surprised, but very frightened. They stayed like this until John finally broke the ice-cold silence. "Yeah. Something was odd about this whole thing."

"Hey!" Vicky tried to defend herself. "You don't believe that there's an actual Interpol agent after a thirteen-year-old girl, do you?"

"What do you think? You came here mysteriously telling us nothing. Then you told us a wacky story, and Paul made us believe in it."

That was when Vicky suddenly jumped on the couch and, standing on it with hands on her waist, directed the attack to

Paul. "Aha! Now it's all about you, Paul."

He lifted up his eyes to the girl and stood up in front of her.

Vicky went on, "Why did you believe me as soon as I got here? You did not even know me."

"What did you want me to do? To be suspicious of such a beautiful girl like you?"

"Humph. So why don't you believe me now?"

"I don't know, okay! I don't know what to believe anymore!"

But Vicky had to stop and think back to what she had just heard. She inquired, not very bravely, if he'd really just used the word *beautiful* to refer to her.

Before Paul could reply, John redirected the subject. "So what do we do now?"

Paul took the piece of paper where the address was written, glanced at it, and showed it to John, telling him what he was told to do. "And he said we're supposed to go alone."

"Meaning you and Vicky," Ringo asked.

Paul nodded, looking down. So George turned to Vicky and asked, "By the way, is your name even Vicky?"

"No! You forgot? It's my nickname."

But George was feeling inquisitive and thought Vicky should elaborate on it.

"That's what my friends call me. You know. Kind of what nicknames are for."

He opened his mouth to ask one more question, but Paul thought that was getting to be too much and stopped him. "George!" And to Vicky, he said, "Vicky, do you have any idea how much trouble you can get us in?"

"Not really," Vicky admitted, looking upset.

"Get *us* in? What do you mean by *us*?" John warned. "Get *you* in! This is *your* house, mate. And I warned you from the beginning that her story was odd."

"Hey, whatever happened to 'I'm beginning to like this bird'?"

Ringo, however, did not like the idea of letting them go by themselves.

"Why not?" John asked of him.

"That's simple. This is all too odd. Okay?"

The girl's eyes shone with hope for a moment. "Ringo, then you believe me?"

"Well, I wish I could, but … "

6 Agent Who?

The moments that followed were tense. Vicky pleaded her case, almost crying, "Why won't you believe me? You trust a voice on the phone more than my word?"

And the guys looked at each other confused.

Around eleven o'clock, they left the house and arrived at the address by midnight. The place was deserted. There was only one car and a person leaning against it. When this person heard the noise and saw the lights of Paul's car, he turned to it. Paul and Vicky got out of the car pretending to be by themselves. He held on tight to her hand. Meanwhile, the others hid inside the car, observing what was about to happen.

The detective called out, "Mr. McCartney?"

"Agent McKenzie?"

"Yes. It's me."

But the closer he got to them, the more Vicky recognized him.

"I see you brought…the girl," he said and looked at Vicky with an evil sneer.

"McKenzie? Are you crazy? You are Gilmar, my teacher! Do you think I look stupid?" She turned to Paul and begged, "Paul, take me away from here! This guy's no agent! He is my former history teacher. Actually, the worst teacher in all history of my school."

"What?"

"Look, I don't know how or why he's here, but it can't be good. If I tell you the things he's done, you won't believe it."

Paul really felt clueless then. He just stood there while McKenzie got closer. Vicky, on the other hand, could not just

41

stand there waiting. She tried to free her arm from his grip but in vain.

"Please, Paul, you gotta believe me! You can't turn me in to Professor Gilmar! I don't know what he wants and—"

"Cut it out, Vicky! You know who I am. Don't start with this professor story." He kept on yelling, this time to Paul, "Hand her over!"

He pulled the girl away so violently that Paul wasn't sure his intentions were that nice anymore. Trying to mend the situation, Gilmar concluded, "Thank you for being a good citizen, Mr. McCartney." Having said that, he turned around and walked toward the car, dragging the girl by her arms.

She kept on calling for Paul. "Paul, help me! You've got to believe me! He is Professor Gilmar! Believe me, please! … Paul!"

Things did not look good for Vicky.

Paul remained standing there, watching the scene. His hands were fidgety inside his pockets.When he finally turned to his car, he hesitated. It was as if his feet were stuck to the ground. That was the moment Gilmar was pushing the girl inside his own car. From that very place, Paul called out, "Professor Gilmar?"

And he answered!

As Paul heard that, he quickly turned and ran toward Gilmar. "You prick! Take your hands off the girl!"

His three other friends got ready to leave the car when they heard that.

When Gilmar saw his disguise go down the drain, he quickly entered the car and tried to start it. Too late! Vicky had already pulled the key out of the ignition and was showing it to him with a smile. So much for being a bragger. Without wasting time, Gilmar thrust her head against the car dashboard.

Paul opened the door. Gilmar jumped on him holding his pocketknife, and the two of them rolled to the ground.

John, followed by George and Ringo, left the car yelling, "You dopey git!" "You prick!" "Let go of my friend!"

Startled, Gilmar dropped the knife, hit Paul in the nose, ran

toward his car, came back for the knife, hurried toward the car again, took the key out of the girl's hand, and started the car. All of that while the others ran toward Paul.

"Are you okay, Paul?" Ringo asked.

"Vicky, mates. We gotta save her from that knobhead!" He replied, trying to get up.

John stopped him. "Don't worry. Stay right there. Ringo, George, go after them. I will stay here with Paul."

George and Ringo jumped in their car and stepped on it. Not too long after that, they were bumper to bumper with Gilmar's car.

"Any ideas?" George asked. "We can't keep this for much longer."

Ringo thought fast and replied, "Keep the speed. I will jump."

George smiled approvingly at the solution, until he realized what Ringo had really just said. "You what? Are you bonkers?"

"Oh, trust me. Stay cool, and get as close as possible to that car."

What could George do? He had asked for an idea. He got as close as possible to the bumper of Gilmar's car.

Without wasting any more time and as carefully as possible, Ringo got out through the window and jumped to the top of

Gilmar's car. All Gilmar heard was a bump on his roof. All he saw were two feet coming through the window right at his face. The two of them began to fight, pushing Vicky against the passenger's seat door. As for the car, it was out of control and on its way off the road.

When Vicky came to and saw that Ringo and Gilmar were fighting while the car was out of control, she panicked and tried to scream. No sound came out of her mouth. She gathered up some courage and decided to put her hands on the wheel. She didn't know how to drive, but, squeezed against the passenger's door and scared to death, she figured she'd try, and put it all in God's hands.

As Gilmar noticed her intention and tried to reach for her arm, Ringo punched him as hard as possible, and he passed out. Ringo pushed him to Vicky's side, took the wheel not very confidently, and smiled at the girl. "I can't drive."

"Oh, cool." She also smiled. But hold on just a second. He had said— "What? Are you crazy, yeah? We're going to die!"

"Not if I can step on the brake."

"So step on the brake! Step on the brake!"

"Well, but I- it- it's not working!"

"Oh, you'd better make it work. Look ahead of us!"

They had gotten off the road and were heading to a cliff straight ahead. They screamed. Ringo slammed on every single pedal, the clutch, the gas, the break, till he finally pulled on the hand brake. The car spun on the grassy terrain and stopped with the back tires off the edge.

Vicky turned her head slowly toward Ringo and, astonished, said, "I thought you said the brake wasn't working."

"Well, you told me to make it work, didn't you."

They laughed, more in relief than to the joke.

George left the car with hands on his head.

"Hey, guys! Are you all right? Come on! Come to our car!"

No one gave it a second thought. They just ran to the car, leaving Gilmar unconscious inside his own car. George then headed to where he had left John and Paul.

That's when Vicky remembered. "Where are Paul and John?"

"We're heading to meet them now," George replied. "John stayed behind to take care of Paul."

"What do you mean? Take care?"

"Yeah, it looks like your teacher punched him in the face."

"What? A punch?" Vicky got excited. "Broke his nose? Is it bleeding? A lot?"

Ringo and George exchanged looks, laughing at the girl's sudden sadism.

"He is okay now. It was not anything really bad."

"Oh, that's too ba—I mean, I mean… " Vicky didn't know what to say. This was the first time someone actually fought for her. She'd only seen things like that in movies, where there was usually a lot a blood involved.

"Don't say anything, young lass," Ringo said. "Do you know what the first thing he said was? 'Oh, mates, go save Vicky!'"

He stared at her, watching her reaction. She smiled an embarrassed smile, like someone who does not know what to do, and after a few seconds in silence, she asked, "Please don't tell Paul what I just said, ok?"

Ringo nodded in agreement.

As soon as the car stopped, Vicky ran toward John and Paul who were sitting on the ground. John got up right away. And the crazy little girl from the car had now changed into a much sober person.

"How is he, John?"

"Well, go ask him."

Vicky, who up until then was a bit tense, got down near Paul with a shy smile and said, "Hey. Hi, Paul."

He responded with a smile. "You got yourself into a heck of a fuss, eh, girl."

"Ay, Paul, I am thirteen! Getting myself in trouble is my specialty!"

Nothing could sound any more logical. Still, everyone thought the remark was funny. Especially because of the serious and solemn face Vicky faked.

"But how are you?"

"I am better now that I see you're okay. But don't bring another teacher like that one here. Those kinds of people make me a bit tired, y'know."

"D'you know he hasn't stopped talking about you?" John observed with a smirk.

Their eyes met for a second. But while Vicky's look was hopeful, Paul's was just hoping she would not have caught up on John's insinuation.

"Yeah, but I think I would feel even better if we could go home now."

The idea was welcomed by all. After all, they were all tired of that little adventure.

But before they could leave, Vicky still told them, "No, guys, let's be serious. Thank you for saving me. Cool?" And, with a grin that went from ear to ear, she added, "Dudes, this was the greatest adventure of all my whole long life experience!"

7 Mommy's Boy

It was about nine-thirty at night when Cláudia, Vítor's mom, got home from work that Friday. As she walked by the play area, she was surprised to see her son lying on the floor near the crazy machine he spent so much time working on. Cláudia ran to him and tried to wake him up.

"Vítor! Vítor! Son! Wake up! Vítor!"

Slowly, he started to open his eyes. Still not sure of what was going on, he asked, "Hmm? What…what happened?"

"I just got home from work. It's way past nine o'clock. And you're here sleeping next to this machine of yours. You must have worked a lot on it today. Don't you think it's better to go upstairs and sleep in your own bed like normal people? You can work tomorrow. "

"Hmm? Oh, okay … all right. Shoot, I can't remember anything at all, and—"

"And where is Vicky? I thought you two were going to be studying for the exams. You need a lot of help with English. You know, you really should leave your little science experiments for summer vacation. It's just a week away. I mean, if you don't fail English. I know you don't like learning languages, but that does not justify…"

Kids in the state of Bahia start taking English as a Foreign Language in fifth grade. Vítor, who could do math with his eyes closed, could not write a sentence in English to save his life. He was in sixth grade, had barely passed the subject the year before, and was about to go to summer school again. Cláudia knew that and was very much worried about her son's plummeting grades. So she went on preaching. But Vítor had zoned out when he heard the sentence "Where is Vicky?"

He directed a desperate look at his mom. "Mom!"

"What? I am serious. You'll need your English to get any decent job in life."

Cláudia had no idea what was going on in the boy's mind, but she noticed that his skin was turning pale and that he had broken into a sweat.

"Vítor? Honey? What happened? You don't look that great. And where is Vicky?"

"Mom! Oh my gosh, Mom!"

"Honey! You listening to me? Did your friend come to study or not?"

Vítor quickly thought of an excuse. "She … couldn't come today. Her … her dad … paid her a surprise visit …"

Vicky's dad lived six hours away and only visited on Children's Day and birthdays. A surprise visit would have been a good reason for skipping a study session. His thinking was perfect. His eyes, however, as well as his mind, were far away, trying to figure out how to fix that mess.

Mom understood those glossy eyes as another sign that he was not well.

"Okay, you know what. Enough of that. I'm taking you to bed immediately. Upstairs. With me. Now!"

"But Mom!"

"No 'but Mom', young man. You're going to bed. And if you're not better tomorrow, I will call Vicky's mom and tell her she can't come at all."

"No! No, no, no! I-I will go to bed. I will be feeling better tomorrow. I promise. Please, don't call Vicky's mom."

"What?"

Okay, Vítor had said something he shouldn't have, and he had to fix it fast. "To tell her not to come!"

"What? Why is that so important? Last I checked, you guys were not dating."

"I really need her help. As you said, I can't fail English. And she does not get math or physics or chemistry without my explaining."

That was true. Vicky was in eighth grade. She had started school two years ahead of Vítor. Even though they were the same age, his mom did not believe in starting school too early. Vicky's family's philosophy was quite the opposite—it's never too early—so she was the youngest in her class. As a result of that, Vicky was already taking physics and chemistry (which she didn't understand at all) while Vítor still had all of seventh grade to go before those subjects were even part of his curriculum. However, he had learned them on his own, and just by looking at Vicky's notes, he knew what they were all about. He was her favorite teacher.

"Okay, I will not tell her mom not to bring her. But you're going to bed right now."

They got up and headed upstairs to their condo. As they climbed the stairs, Mom kept on going. "Did you even eat anything? It's probably lack of food. You know how we say, 'an empty bag can't stay up'."

Vítor looked back at his machine with some hope, thinking that, at least, Gilmar had not taken it with him. He probably did not realize there was such an option. That would have been a total disaster.

"So before bed, a good shower and a nutritious dinner. You're really pale. That's worrying me. Then a delightful night of sleep so that tomorrow you and Vicky can get some studying done. Did she say what time she'll come?"

"Uh, early. Early...in...in the morning."

"Okay, I will leave for work at six. Your dad won't be home tomorrow either, so I sent your sisters to Grandma's. You guys will be on your own. Don't eat junk food all day. Don't read comics all day. And no trips to the mall. There are oranges and bananas in the fruit basket. Don't let the fruit go bad."

"Okay, okay. We won't."

"Ah, why do I not believe you!"

Vítor was relieved. He grinned at the prospect of not having grownups or nosy little sisters around. Not having to come up with excuses would make his life easier. He knew exactly what to do now. And he would do it without being questioned or looked for.

8 *The Early Bird*

The next morning, Vicky woke up early and got herself dressed up. Having found nothing to do, she decided to sit on the couch and wait for everyone else to rise. That's when she saw Paul, who had gotten up just a couple of minutes after her and was fixing up his hair with his hands.

"Hi, Paul."

"Good morning, Vicky. Did you sleep well?"

"I did, thank you. Hey, no one else is up yet. Want to sit down over here with me while I braid my hair?"

"Sure."

Paul sat by her side, and both of them turned to face each other. Vicky started braiding tight skinny braids with thin chunks of hair.

"You're going to do that to all of your hair?"

"Nah, just a couple here and there. To look different. People in my school think it's cool. They like to copy me. Every time I go to school like that, the girls start braiding their hair during recess. I like when people copy me."

"I would not want to do that in my hair."

Vicky giggled at that remark. "You would look funny." She looked down then looked back at Paul and said, "It was really cool what you did yesterday."

"You think? I almost let you go with that knobhead."

"*Almost*, old man. That makes a difference."

"Vicky, why do you keep calling us old men? I mean, I know you're just a little girl, but we're not really old, y'know. I'm

51

twenty-one. I mean—"

"I keep calling you what? *Oxe*! No!" Vicky chuckled. "I don't mean you're- No! No no no! That's just- that's just the way I talk. I call everyone old man. I call my best friend old man. And my brother. And my—believe me, old man, I don't think you're old."

"Oh. Okay. So you just talk funny."

"What?"

"Oxe – you say *oxe* all the time. What is that supposed to mean?"

"You talk funny too."

"No, I don't."

"You do. You guys say *mate* and *odd* and *are-eh*. Dude! You talk funny! *Are-eh* – the heck is that supposed to mean?"

"That's our scouse accent!"

"Whatever. Anyway, thanks for saving me from Professor Creep. I don't even know what would have happened. I was so scared!"

"Well, now you're back with us, safe and sound."

"And you too, right?" She smiled. "How's your nose?"

"Yeah, about that. I was told you have been laughing at me."

"I have what? Ringo told you? Ay, Paul, come on! You did not take that seriously, right?"

Paul raised his eyebrows with a smile and shrugged.

"Ay, ay, ay…okay, maybe I am watching too many movies."

"Maybe you are."

Vicky double-checked. Was everyone else was still asleep? Well, that was interesting. She did not think twice. That was the moment she had been hoping for. She disguised a smile, ran her hand through his hair, and tried to kiss him. But Paul cut her fun short by holding her hand.

"Whoa, Vicky, hold on. There's something wrong here."

She pretended not to understand him. "What?"

"Don't you think you're going way too fast? You're a child. Shouldn't you wait a few years?"

"Paul, you don't get it. It's just that … it's not about my growing up, it's that … well, I'll never … we'll never …"

Vicky decided to stop talking. Any explaining would ruin her plan. She stared at him silently and, without wasting any more time, kissed him.

Truth be told, that was not a kiss like those she'd seen on TV or anything like that. It was more what you'd call a lip-lock, which was probably the only thing she knew how to do. But John happened to wake up in time to watch it, rub his eyes, look again, and say, "Paul? Vicky? Already?" And he smirked like an annoying older brother would.

Paul, startled, tried to justify himself. "I-I did not- we were only- sh-sh-she was the one who … uh …"

"Sure, blame it all on the bird."

Paul looked at Vicky upset, but she did not seem to mind. She hit her forehead with her hand, and said, "Paul, don't say anything, okay? You're going to ruin it. Besides, are you going to listen to this goofball?"

John threw a plain glance at Vicky and concluded, "*Are-eh,* you are odd!"

"Who? Me? Go figure."

9 Scrambled Eggs After Breakfast

The talk around breakfast time was of the incident the night before.

"Vicky," Ringo asked, "who is this Professor Gilmar?"

"Oh, he's a teacher I had. He has a few loose screws. He did not really like me because my friends and I made a point of turning his life into a living hell," she explained while finishing her scrambled eggs and toast. "Actually, no one at the Ruy Barbosa Institute really liked him. By no one, I mean, the students, because the teachers... You how that goes, right?"

"Right," John said. "But what do you think he wanted from you?"

"To be honest, I did not think he remembered me anymore because it's been a very long time since I have seen him. But it might be revenge."

"Revenge?" George was confused.

"He was kicked out of school because of me."

"Say that again?" Ringo said.

Vicky explained, spitting out words faster than she could think, "Well, my gang and I found out, totally by chance, some nasty stuff about him, and we made sure the administration found out. But he found out I was involved in the whole story. See, I was never afraid like the rest of the gang. I just made all the grownups think I never did anything wrong. That's, like, my specialty – making grownups think I'm a little angel. That's why I was always covering for my gang. But then I made myself an easy target."

"You're so inconsequential," John said as soon as she paused to breathe.

"Yeah…that." Then she went on, "But so what? I was always the number one student in that class. In all my classes, by the way. I skipped class every now and then, but big deal. Every one thought there was a good reason behind everything I did in that school. That was why he hated me. He could not get even with me because he had no opportunity for it. That's why Mom pulled me out of that school. She was afraid I was going to turn into some juvenile delinquent."

"Yes, but when you made him leave the school…" Ringo was hoping she'd continue the story, still dizzy with Vicky's speedy speech.

"All I knew was that because of that story, his life was pretty much over. And that was because of my gang. Yes, because he knows I did not do things by myself. But he can only be suspicious of the others. He does not know who they are. But I had not seen him since that thing happened. I had even forgotten all about it."

"It seems he hadn't, doesn't it?" Ringo said.

"Yeah ..." she replied with a sigh.

Vicky and her gang did drive the history teacher crazy. She hadn't told the guys half the story. Let's just say that by "turning his life into a living hell," she really meant things like pouring artificial vomit mix made up of Nesquik, mashed banana, flour, eggs, tomatoes, spaghetti, ketchup, mayo, mustard, powdered milk and prune yogurt on the teacher's head – all the way down from the second floor of the school building. This wacky mix could not have come from anywhere other than the twisted minds of that crazy girl and her accomplices. Gilmar had just walked into the school and was almost to the teachers' lounge when that happened. All the other teachers saw the scene and, once he was out of sight, cracked up.

"What was it that you discovered about him anyway?" Ringo inquired.

"Well, uh … he was … taking, like, 'favors' from girl students to give them passing grades."

"Oh boy."

"Yeah."

"And you had hoped he'd have forgotten about what you guys did?"

"I am surprised he is not in jail," John pointed out.

"Me too. But I just don't understand how he ended up here."

"Why not?"

"Because there's no way anyone from where I live can come here. Only Vítor could bring someone from there to here. And Vítor would not do that to me. At least I … I think that's the case. Right?"

"Vicky, what a wacky story! Isn't Vítor just a boy? How can he be the only one who can—"

"Wait, John. Stop right there. This conversation is going too far. Remember our deal?"

"You're odd."

As that conversation died down, Vicky's eyes looked for Paul. He was quiet, away from that whole chat.

"Paul?"

"Hmm?" he said.

"You okay?"

"Sure."

"You look like you're on another planet."

"I was just thinking."

"Thinking? About what?"

"Well, sometimes we have to stop and think about the things that have happened, y'know. And … Vicky, there is something odd about you, I can't deny that. But I can tell you're cool. I will not be suspicious of you anymore. Okay?"

Her smile went from ear to ear. "That's awesome."

Then she looked at the same piano she had noticed the night before. She got up, walked to it, played two keys, and asked Paul, "You play the piano, don't you?"

"Yes, I do. You?"

"Me? Ay, ay. I wish. I only play the recorder, and not that well."

"The recorder? Do you like playing it?"

"Yeah… What I hate is having to practice the music my teacher has me play."

"But why?"

"Old man! *Having* to do anything is very boring. Anything. Besides, *caramba*! I wish I could play something people know, like Chitãozinho & Xororó or Sandy & Junior, whom, by the way, I like. But then the teacher tells me to play some "Tanzlied" which neither I nor anyone knows. That is so boring! Then all my friends at school laugh at me."

"Who's Chitãozinho & Xororó? And Sandy & Junior?"

"Chitãozinho & Xororó are country singers I like. Sandy & Junior are their children, and they also sing. They've been singing since they were, like, three years old."

"Country singers! You're American! Aren't you?"

"Hey! No! America is not the only place to have country singers, you know. I'm not telling you where I'm from till tomorrow."

"Are-eh, fine. But you should practice, y'know. Have you tried learning by ear?"

She stared at him as if studying his words, sliding her hands on the piano. Then she chuckled, dismissing the suggestion, "No."

"What you laughing at? That's how I've learned."

"And that's why you're Paul McCartney. You can do anything. Me? I'm just Vicky. I'm good at stuff like English, and Portug- I-I mean history! … History, and geography, and civics and… devising evil plans to trick grownups into thinking I'm an angel…"

Those final words themselves were an evil plan quickly designed to divert Paul's attention to the fact that she had almost given out the word Portuguese as her mother tongue, which might end up leading to more inquiries about where she'd come from. But she had lost him on "You can do anything."

Paul just shook his head a little uneasy, chuckled, and mentioned to Ringo, "Mate, fans are exaggerated." And to Vicky, "Okay, Vicky, whatever you say," and kept on eating.

She was still standing there thinking that was a close call, when Paul finished up his breakfast. As soon as he was done, Vicky pleaded, "Paul, will you play me something?"

He looked at her, smiled, and walked toward the piano.

"I will."

Paul sat at the piano, played a whole scale, and then asked the girl what song she would like to hear. Good question. What should she say? She had drawn a blank on all pre-1964 songs at that moment. She thought of "Hey Jude," "The Long and Winding Road," "Let It Be," but they were all post-1964. She did not even want to suggest "Yesterday."

Her indecisive face led Paul to just say, "Can't think of anything?"

Vicky shook her head.

"Well, then… Let's try something new."

Paul looked at the keyboard for a moment and began to play a beautiful melody on his piano. And that was "Yesterday".

At the end of the execution, she exclaimed, "Wow, Paul! This is my favorite song, you know."

"You've heard it before?"

"No! No! I just … I just … I really liked it, just by hearing it … n-now … as you played it. Y'know."

"Oh. Okay. … Are you sure you've never heard it before? Not even something similar?"

"Positive."

"Brilliant. I just woke up with this melody in my mind. I haven't got the lyrics for it yet, but I'm glad you like it. I guess I could call it … 'Sweet…Curly…Girl'?"

Vicky was not sure what he meant. After all, wasn't that "Yesterday"? She began to repeat the words without realizing what Paul had meant. "Sweet Curly…" When she understood the meaning of that title, she could barely believe it. "Paul! Is this song for me? For me?"

His smile was the answer she needed.

"Play it again!"

Paul played it once more and that's when it hit her. Now she really had altered history! That was indeed "Yesterday." She had read that Paul had woken up with the melody in his mind one morning. But … it was never called "Sweet Curly Girl." Its early title was "Scrambled Eggs." Vicky tried to fix that little historical glitch she got herself into. "You know, those scrambled eggs sure were good! Don't you think? I mean, wow! They were good! Right?"

"Yeah. S-sure. They were good."

"No, but really! Scrambled eggs are, like, the best food ever! Don't you think?"

Paul couldn't possibly catch up on that weird talk, so he asked Vicky if she would like to learn how to play the piano.

"M-m-me?"

"Yes, you. Is there any other Vicky around here?"

"Well, I…I don't think I can, Paul."

"I don't think I can, Paul," he mocked her with a little-kid voice. Then he went on with a serious face, "Well, of course you can, little girl. Come here."

There's no doubt that was a delightful morning. Paul tried to teach Vicky to play the piano, and after a while, she was able to play a few notes for the introduction of one Beatles song she hadn't learned yet: "You Really Got a Hold on Me." John liked that and sang the first line. Paul sang the second one, and the others joined in. And they ended up playing several songs upon Vicky's request, like "Little Child," "Devil in Her Heart," and "Chains." Vicky was delighted and took every chance she had to ask anything that came to her mind about them.

~~~~MEANWHILE~~~~IN~~~~1993 ~~~~

Vítor was sitting inside the machine thinking, hands supporting his forehead and hair hanging on the dashboard.

"The whole automated setting to bring Vicky back has been messed with. It won't bring her back anymore. The only way out is traveling there myself. At least I have the option to locate the last people that were in here. I just have to make sure it takes me to Vicky and not to Gilmar."

What if it would actually take him to Gilmar instead? And what if the machine really could not find his friend? And what if Gilmar had done something to her? And what if… Poor kid! All those questions were making his mind spin.

"Okay. I've got to do this now. No more what-ifs. I will take the machine and go pick her up. Hop off, grab her by the arm, hop back on, gone. If she screams or kicks, she'll come kicking and screaming." He let out a sigh and raised his eyes to heaven. "God, don't let it be too late. Please."

Vítor checked his watch. It was a little bit past nine in the morning. He'd get there close to twelve-thirty. He closed the hatch, buckled up, and turned a key. The machine started to spin faster and faster till it disappeared.

10 *Blinking lights And Colorful Buttons*

~~~~ 1993 ~~~~1990 ~~~~1984 ~~~~1980~~~~
~~~~1974 ~~~~1970 ~~~~1964 ~~~~

The machine arrived spinning inside Paul's house, along with lightning and a lot of wind. The spinning became slower and slower until it stopped. No one had a clue of what was going on until Vicky saw the hatch open and Vítor pop out of it, as dizzy as if he had been inside a spinning top. She was astonished.

"Vítor?"

When the guys heard that, they looked at her, surprised.

Vítor stopped and tried to keep his balance. Everything was spinning in his mind. There was nothing else he could do – he went face-first on the floor. Vicky and the guys ran to him.

"So *this* is Vítor?" Ringo asked, turning the boy's body so that he was lying on his back.

"Yup."

George studied his face and made a comment. "He does look like Paul."

"Like me?" Yes, he did. Paul could not deny that. He made an annoyed face and asked Vicky, "Your boyfriend?"

"Just because he looks like you?"

John did not care to comment on that. He looked at the machine, got up, walked around it, and signaled to George, who asked, "What is that?"

That? That was simple; it meant trouble ahead. But Vicky was not about to put herself on the line, so she passed the hot potato to her friend. "I think Vítor can explain anything better than me, George."

"Did you come here in this thing?" Ringo asked her.

Vicky looked at him as one who could not speak the language and said nothing else. Paul asked George to go grab the ammonia to get the boy to come to.

When Vítor came to and saw himself on the floor surrounded by the Beatles, he was stupefied. He sat up and pulled himself backward.

"Hey, Vítor, calm down!" Vicky said, sitting right behind him and holding his shoulder. "Look, they are the Beatles. See? Here's Ringo Starr, George Harrison, and Paul McCartney."

As for John, he was inside the machine.

But the boy did not seem to care for the fact that he was right in front of the Fab Four.

"Huh? Oh, yes. Of course. Vicky, I came to bring you back. We have a problem. We have to go back to ninety-three *right*

now!"

Vicky did not like what she heard. She jumped up to her feet and complained, "What? Now? But you said two days!"

"I know, but—"

"No! No way, Ray! I do not want to go back to ninety-three. I want to stay right here in sixty-four until tomorrow, as we agreed on." She was really very annoyed.

"But, Vicky," Vítor desperately tried to explain himself, "you're not getting it. We *must* go back *now*!"

"And why is that?" She questioned him with arms crossed and with an aggravated face.

Before Vítor could organize his answer, Paul, who, along with his two other pals, had no idea what was going on, asked, "Hey, hold on there, you two. What are you talking about? Ninety-three? Sixty-four? Is this some kind of code language? ... Are-eh, these crazy Americans!"

"*We're not American!*" the two children replied.

At this moment, John came out from inside the machine. "Mate, you're awake. Listen- wow, don't you look like Paul!" he mentioned with a grin.

"We know that already, Johnny." Paul said impatiently.

So John went on. "Listen, what is this loony machine you have here filled with devices, numbers, and blinking lights?"

As he heard that, Vítor directed a frightened look to Vicky, as if asking for help.

"Yeah, Vítor, I think you have a lot of explaining to do to this gang here. I alone could never have ruined things as fast as you did."

"Er ... w-well ... it's that—"

"Wait, you ill-mannered boy!" Vicky interrupted him. "First, introductions. This is John Lennon. Boys, this is Vítor."

"Vicky told us about you. And how you look like Paulie here."

Vítor directed a sad grin to John, and Paul asked him to explain at once what was going on. Vítor gathered up his courage, stood up, took a deep breath, explained, "Simple! *This* is a time machine. And *you* are coming back with *me* to the year nineteen ninety-three." and pulled the girl by the hand.

She opposed him one more time, and Paul asked, trying to make sense of it all, "Wait a second. Time machine? Ninety-three? Nineteen ninety-three, is what you said? You mean you came from the year nineteen ninety-three?"

"What?" John did not believe he understood it.

"So we'll still be famous in nineteen ninety-three?" Ringo asked. But just because that was all he could ask after listening to such an absurd statement.

"Well, I am not sure of that, but you are *my* favorite stars," said Vicky.

Vítor insisted once again, but Vicky did not accept his order. And Paul was still not buying the machine story.

"Vicky, you're not explaining this thing right. I mean, you're joking, right? You came from the future?"

"Of course. Why else would I make so much secret about where I came from?"

Paul still held a smile of disbelief. "Who knows, so many reasons. Mate, this is nonsense, okay. I mean—"

"You still don't believe it."

"No, I don't believe it. Can you prove it?"

Everyone was silent. Paul thought he had ended that little made-up story. After a little thinking, however, Vicky found a way to solve two problems at once. "Well, you guys, how about we do some time traveling? What do you say, Paul?"

"Time traveling? Do you have to take any wacky pills first?" he asked her.

"No!"

He still looked at her, not knowing what to believe. Shaking his head, he announced, "Okay. Sign me up. I'm going to see the future."

However, someone else in the room did not like the idea.

"What? Vicky, don't you start! There's…there isn't even any room in the machine. It was built for two. Two children."

"Whattup, Vítor? Don't you be a party pooper!" And to

reinforce her plea, she hit her right fist against her left hand, her *persuasive technique*.

Vítor looked at her, annoyed, and gave up. "Okay, if it is for the welfare of all and general felicity of the gang...[5] Oh, I have no say in it anyways."

The guys laughed at the way the girl had control over her friend.

"I knew you would understand me, *sweetie pea*," she replied.

Now Vítor had to figure out how to fit everyone inside the machine. Luckily, there were lots of handlebars. They were not meant for holding extra people, but they would do. A little while later, everyone was already inside the machine horsing around as Vítor pushed buttons, and set up all the time coordinates. Trying to actually move in there and actually see the buttons he was pushing was not as simple as it had been before, without four extra bodies above the maximum capacity. Then he turned a key, and the machine began to spin.

But wait a second! Something was wrong! Of course! With all the mess inside his machine, Vítor made a mistake. He tried punching in 1993, and he thought he had set the right place. But the year entered was not 1993, and the place was never set.

5Famous words by the Prince of Brazil in the 1820s on the day his father, the King of Portugal, required him to go back to Portugal: "If it is for the welfare of all and the general felicity of the nation, tell the people I'll stay!" Today it is used whenever someone is giving in to peer pressure.

11 *Somewhere In The Past*

~~~~~ ~~~~~ ~~~~~ ~~~~~ ~~~~~

When the machine stopped spinning, they all stayed in there for a few minutes, waiting for the rest of the world to stop spinning, as Vicky had suggested. Finally, as everyone was ready to get out, she noticed something strange as she peeked outside through one of the two small windows Vítor had been careful to add to the machine.

"Vítor, where are we again?"

"What?"

She opened the hatch and hopped outside, saying, "This looks nothing like Brazil and nothing like nineteen ninety-three."

At that moment, a little boy was about to zoom by her. She thrust herself in front of the kid, making him bump into her.

"Kiddo, what year are we in?"

That's not the kind of question people usually ask. The boy thought he had not understood it. "What? Out of my way!" he screamed in excitement.

"Wait, Tiny! Where are you going in such a hurry? What place is this?"

"Judea, everybody knows it. Now let me go, I'm trying to go see Jesus."

"What? Jesus? He is really here?"

"If you won't let go of me, he'll not be anywhere anymore by the time I get there."

Vicky froze as she heard that but did not let go of the little boy's arm.

"Let me go!" he cried.

"Wait! Kiddo, I have a surprise for you. But only if you take me with you to see Jesus. But wait just a second. I have to tell my friends that I am leaving."

"Oh, okay. But go quickly."

Vicky raced back to the machine. Everyone was staring at her looking frightened. Vítor gave her the news she already knew. "Vicky, I-I set the numbers wrong. We're in the year AD twenty-eight. B-but I will fi—"

"I know, my love. And do you know who's right over there? Jesus Christ himself. And I am going there to meet him, and you're not stopping me, okay. Good-bye and that's it."

She ran away, and Vítor ran after her, followed by the other guys, who were eager to get out of the egg they had been in for the past few minutes.

"But we must go back to nineteen ninety—"

"We'll do that later! We've got plenty of time!" she yelled from afar. Then she turned back to him and went on. "I must go do the crazy things young people must do!" And she started running again to catch up to the little kid she had met.

"Crazy things young people must do?" Paul repeated. "What on earth does she think she is talking about?"

"We ended up in Jesus Christ's time," John thought out loud.

"Exactly. And since there was no place set, the machine brought us to the most important known historical event of the time. Modesty aside, my machine is just perfect."

"I have to go see that." John said and took off in the same direction Vicky went.

"Wait! Come back here! Where are you going?" Vítor said and sighed. "Oh, this is going to set us back." He looked very annoyed.

George, however, thought differently. "Why don't we all go?"

"What was that?"

"Vítor, the person over there is none other than Jesus Christ. He's no one important, just the bloke responsible for the change in the way we count time in human history. He's someone important, whatever belief you might have. You can't just waste the chance to meet the man in person."

"Oh no. Listen, George. I'm sorry. I don't even really know you guys that well. I don't want to sound like I'm complaining, but it's my machine. Is that clear? The people that go in it are the people I want in it, when I allow it, and they go or do what I decide they can go or do. Is that clear?"

"Oh, really?" Paul took offense for his friend. "Not the impression I got, mate. It looked to me like Vicky tells you what you can and can't do with *your* machine."

"Hey, dude, you stay in your place! My problem with Vicky is something I deal with!"

"Whoa! I will not be here arguing with little ones. Excuse me." Paul said that and started walking toward where Vicky had gone. "George, you coming or not?"

George followed him.

"Hey! Get back here!" Vítor said and followed them.

Ringo figured he would not be the one left standing there. He was in for the ride too.

Paul found John observing the crowd at a safe distance. He stopped next to him and watched the scene as well. George and Vítor soon caught up to them and stood there watching the same scene. Just two years later, John would affirm the Beatles were more popular than Jesus Christ and cause a lot of commotion. What he really meant, only God knows. He later apologized for maybe having been misunderstood. But he probably started thinking about it right there in the year AD 28.

"You're not going there, John?" George asked.

"I don't think so," he replied, still pensive, not able to take his eyes off the crowd.

Ringo soon arrived where they were.

"Why are we not moving?"

Vítor started apologetically to Paul. "Look, I … did not mean to be rude, but—"

"But you were. That's cool."

"Dude, you, like, don't get it. Do you know the only reason why I spent months building this machine? So that Vicky could

go and meet the Beatles … and you, of course."

Paul could not disguise a smile.

"I only built the machine because of her. I just wish she'd understand … It's not just the machine … I'd do anything for her."

"Oh. You're in love with her. Aren't you?" Paul asked, as if beginning to figure things out.

"Nah, not anymore. When I began building the machine, yes. We dated for a while. But we're just friends now. I got tired of looking 'exactly like Paul McCartney' all the time."

"Like me?"

"Like, Vicky is just weird, dude. It's a thirty-eight-year difference between the two of you. But I think you're the only person she really likes."

John laughed as he heard that.

Paul shrugged. "That's just what I needed."

While the guys were having this deep conversation, the girl and the little boy were already on their way back.

"What are you all standing here for? Let's go?"

"Well, did you see him?" George asked.

"I did. Old man, there were so many people there, I couldn't get too close! But I got this little guy to go and talk to him, since he was talking to children."

"You do realize you are a child, right?" John said with a smirk. "You could have gone."

"Who? Me? A kid? No, I'm a teenager. Almost an adult," she said that with a dissimulated look to Paul who pretended not to have noticed that.

Paul, actually, couldn't get his eyes off Vítor. Yes, they looked alike, but that wasn't what he was thinking about. So Vítor and Vicky *had* dated. So he was right all along. Vítor *was* her boyfriend. Well, ex-boyfriend. But second of all, he still liked her. Oh yes, he did. Oh, the poor kid.

Vítor, on the other hand, couldn't get his eyes off the boy, which eventually made the little boy uncomfortable.

"Vicky ... who is the kid?"

"He took me there. His name is Joshua. Joshua, these are my friends Vítor, Ringo, George, John, and Paul."

"Nice to meet you," he said.

They all acknowledged him with hi's and hello's, but Vítor directed a worried glance at Vicky.

"I thought I had to reward the kiddo, Vítor. But don't worry. He is only going to *see* the machine."

"Argh, let's just go," Vítor said.

As they got to the machine, Vicky began to explain. "Look, Tiny, what I will say will sound absurd to you, but I guarantee you can believe it. First, look at this machine."

Joshua looked at the Magic Vítor inside and out, not able to understand it at all. But he was pretty amazed by the looks of it.

"What is this thing?"

"This is a time machine, kiddo. Do you know what you do with it?"

The boy shook his head. Vicky went on, "You can travel to the future or to the past as if they were today."

"Huh? Witchcraft?"

"Nope, just science. We traveled almost two thousand years from the future, from a country that doesn't even exist yet called Brazil."

Meanwhile, Vítor was getting the others inside. Of course, this time he had set the right time and place while everyone was outside. He had learned his lesson.

"But how- So you guys came from the future to meet Jesus?"

Vicky was a little embarrassed because that was far from being the reason they were there.

"Well, sort of."

Joshua looked inside the machine, and when he saw everyone in there, he felt something little kids feel regardless of the year or millennium they are born in. "Oh, please let me travel with you a little bit."

Vicky felt sorry for the little guy, but she had to explain to him that the owner of the machine was a perfect idiot and would not let that happen. Joshua directed a sad look to Vítor, who was inside the machine waiting for Vicky. He thought that guy was probably the worst dictator in the history of mankind. Then he looked down, resigned.

"Vicky, let's go." Vítor yelled from the machine.

Vicky looked at one boy then at the other. She had to think fast. She put her hands inside her pocket and found, by chance, a little square made with window grout, in which she had written Vicky Was Here. She had made it when she was at a friend's house. The house was being remodeled and there was extra grout all over the place. But, being a kid herself, she knew that little kids loved these little otherwise-meaningless tokens.

"Hey, take this little window grout piece with you. This way you can remember me."

As she noticed that he was trying to read it, she explained, "It says 'Vicky was here' in English."

Joshua smiled a sad and embarrassed smile for having no idea what English was and handed to her something to remind herself of him—a piece of wood with his name engraved in Aramaic.

"My father made it. I can always ask him for another one."

"Your father made it?"

"He is a carpenter."

"Cool. Thanks."

"Vicky!" Vítor called out again.

Vicky looked at him and quickly turned back to Joshua.

Vicky looked at Vítor quickly, and bid Joshua farewell, running her hand through his hair, then went into the machine. She closed the hatch and waved to the boy.

Everything had been checked. There could be no mistakes this time. Vítor turned the machine on, and it began to spin faster and faster until it was gone. Joshua watched all that in amazement, and after a few seconds standing there, he ran away.

12 *Private Tutoring*

~~~128 ~~~452~~~762 ~~~1128 ~~~1453~~~1789 ~~~
~~~1890~~~1964 ~~~1993~~~

At last, the machine was back to 1993 in Brazil. Now Vicky was sure they were in the play area of Vítor's condo, which she had left less than twenty-four hours ago.

"We are in nineteen ninety-three, Salvador, Bahia, gang," Vítor announced.

Vicky tried to tell them to wait until no one was dizzy anymore, but this time it did not work. Paul claimed no one could breathe in there anymore. Ringo claimed he could no longer feel his legs. Everyone was ready to get out, even if still dizzy. So everyone started getting out. That's when they heard a voice.

"Oh my. I thought you were not coming back."

Vítor's and Vicky's hearts jumped out their mouths. They jumped back, slamming against John, George, Ringo, and Paul. The guys thought the children had seen a ghost. They had actually seen...

"Hi, Aunt Cláudia," Vicky said in a monotone, realizing there really wasn't anywhere to run.

"Mom," Vítor said, trying to smile, having no idea how to mend the situation. "Vicky's here."

"That's right. I was about to call her mom. Maybe I should have. What are you guys doing? And who are your new friends?"

Vítor heard a voice behind his head.

"I take it you did not tell your old lady you'd have us over for dinner." That was John, trying to make a joke out of Vítor's soon-to-be-over life.

"Mom—"

"Aunt Cláudia! These are João, Paulo, Jorge, and Ricardo. They are private tutors. My mom hired them. We used Vítor's cool machine to go get them."

Cláudia was not buying that. "Private tutors? Since when do you need private tutors? And why didn't she tell me about this over the phone?"

"Because—"

"Because it was her dad's idea. All her dad's idea, Mom. You know. Her dad. He gave her mom the money to hire these guys this morning."

Cláudia looked at the four "tutors". They were striving to keep a serious face.

"You guys are tutors?"

"Yes, ma'am," John agreed.

"What do you teach?"

The children froze.

"Uh, math, chemistry, physics, and English." John said quickly, pointing to each of his pals as he said each subject.

Lucky guess. Exactly what the kids had said they'd be studying. Very lucky guess.

"Fine," she said, thinking of the next question. "Where did Suely find you?"

Suely was Vicky's mom. None of the guys knew that. So Vítor saved the day. "At UFBA. It's a tutoring program they have."

"Oh, the UFBA Solidary Education Program. My goodness, I've heard of that. You guys are expensive."

Another lucky guess. Vítor had never heard of a UFBA Solidary Education Program. UFBA was the local federal university, and neither Vítor nor Vicky felt they were old enough to bother paying attention to anything related to it.

"What can I say? We're the best." George surprised everyone by joining the game.

"Yeah, yeah. You know what? Vicky's father is paying you. I don't care. The guy is never there for his kids, and when he decides to show up, he thinks nothing is good enough." And to her son, she said, "Vítor, I came home to check on your fever. But you look fine. I'm going upstairs to eat lunch. I can fix you guys something."

"Uh, no, Mom, we grabbed McDonald's. That's where we're coming from right now."

"You all did?"

Everyone replied with a yes.

Cláudia sighed. "Why do I bother trying to make you eat healthy? I'm going upstairs. You guys don't take too long down here. Half the day is gone already. Tutors make no miracle."

"Okay, Mom. We will cover the machine and meet you up there in a minute."

Cláudia started her way toward the stairs, and everyone got ready to breathe. But then she turned back and looked at them again, as if she had noticed something. She looked at George and said, "You look like my husband."

"Oh, really?"

"Yeah, really. Anyone ever told you you look like George Harrison from the Beatles? That's why I started dating him. George was my favorite Beatle."

"Oh, thank you." Everyone looked at George as if trying to remind him he was not supposed to be George. But he knew that. He went on, "But no, no one ever said that to me."

She turned around and went upstairs.

They watched her go, holding a heavy silence, the kind of silence that will disappear into laughter at any moment.

When she was gone, Paul mocked, "You look like George Harrison from the Beatles!"

Everyone cracked up, and the silence was gone.

"João, Paulo, Jorge, and Ricardo. Vicky, you're da beast!" Vítor screamed.

"What are these names, Vicky?" Paul asked.

"They are your names in Portuguese. What about John? John, you said the exact four subjects we have to study for. You could play the lottery today."

"And the UFBA- what was it? Soli-" Vítor tried.

"Solidary," Vicky helped.

"Right, Education program."

"Did you know about that?"

"No."

"We could win the lottery today!"

When the laughter died down, Ringo said, "You guys, you never told your parents anything about this, did you?"

"No!" Vicky and Vítor said, looking at Ringo as if he had suggested something completely absurd.

"And we're not about to say anything now. We'll be grounded for life." Vítor added.

John asked, "Vicky, didn't you say you only had your mum? How come Vítor said your dad hired us?"

Vicky just stared at him and did not answer right away. John began to wonder if he should have asked that question at all. She finally replied, "Because I really only have my mom." She looked down. Then, not wanting to ruin the fun, she turned to Paul and explained, "That's it, Paul. The future."

"So, am I still alive in the future? What happened to me?"

"Yeah, you're still alive. You're fifty-one, married, and have four children."

Paul was not sure. how to react to that. He just said, "Wow…n-nice to know that."

"What about me?" John asked.

"You?" Vicky gasped. "... your son is a singer." And that's when she remembered one tiny detail. "All right. Now, Mister Vítor, you're turning out to be a very responsible guy. First of all, you take every one of us to the beginning of the first millennium. Now just explain to me, what was Gilmar doing in nineteen sixty-four?"

Vítor tripped over his words while trying to find an explanation.

"Vicky, it was not really my fault—"

"Oh, it was not your fault. That's what they all say!"

"Did he cause you any trouble?" he asked in a tiny voice, the one he used whenever Vicky yelled at him.

"If he caused me any trouble? No, of course not. Go figure. If he caused me any trouble. Humph!"

Vítor had begun to put together a relieved smile when...

"You'll be the one in trouble when I get my hands on you!"

She grabbed him by the shirt collar against the marble pillar.

"Dude! Chill, Vicky, chill! I can explain. I-I-I-I can explain."

"Explain what, old man?"

Vítor clarified the whole story. Then Vicky had no choice but to apologize to her friend. After all, she had been just as careless as he had about keeping the machine a secret. But Vítor did not pass on the teasing. "It's all right. I know you have a bad temper."

"What? You… Oh, I want to break your face in two sometimes."

Ringo, George, and John were laughing at that whole circus. Paul, however, wasn't really listening or even seeing them. He was thinking about what he had heard a few seconds before. So in 1993 he was married? That was crazy talk. That was… Wait! What was that all about then? He immediately mouthed to John that they should get going.

"Hey, mates, not meaning to interrupt anything," John tried to draw attention to himself, "we have to get back to nineteen sixty-four."

"You're … leaving already?" Vicky directed a startled look to Paul. "But you just got here. Why are you leaving so soon? Why won't you stay longer?"

"We can't. We have to go back to nineteen sixty-four and move on with our lives. Isn't that true?"

"But, Paul, stay a little longer."

"Vicky, that's not a good idea."

"Oh, isn't it sad to separate such a cute couple, mates?" John joked.

"What are you saying, Lennon?" Vítor asked.

Paul, however, did not want to hear any more of that gossip and got back to his subject. "So, Vítor, can you send us back to nineteen sixty-four?"

"In a second."

"Stay a little while longer with us," Vicky insisted. "You guys just got here."

"Yeah, Paul. Why the rush?" Ringo also asked.

"Well. You know. It's sort of odd to feel so far away from your own time."

But that did not convince anyone.

Vicky kept thinking, *how hard can they make this?*

But one thing was true: when this girl wanted anything that had to do with the Beatles, she did not waste any time. She'd come up with any sort of plan, as lame as it could be, but she'd come up with something. She took advantage of the fact that Vítor was inside the machine and said, "Look, gang, while you are still here, I want your autographs in my datebook."

"Of course." Ringo replied. "It will be our pleasure."

But that was not exactly what Vicky really had in mind.

While the guys were busy with her datebook, she whispered to them, "Look, gang, Vítor is not really a fan of you guys. I mean, today there's heavy metal, which is different than your kind of music. And the boys today are more into that. If you stay a little longer and he gets to know you, maybe he'll change his mind. What do you say, Ringo?"

Ringo glanced at George and asked the others, "What d'you say?"

"Rubbish, Vicky." Paul complained. "Who cares what Vítor likes?"

"But, Paul. I thought… Okay," she started again, holding his arm, "Look, stay just one more day. There's so much to see and do in nineteen ninety-three! Don't you see how much fun it will be? Tonight you guys can go back to the same May 1 you left from."

Ringo agreed. "Yes, mates, let's go walk around. It will be fun."

Paul, for a few seconds, watched her with a pensive look.

Ringo went on, "Well, what's the rush? We have a time machine. We have all the time we want!"

Paul glanced at John. John seemed to like the idea.

"Stop being silly, you two. Oh my, John, I thought you were more fun driven. You never looked the nerdy type." John looked inquisitively at Paul and asked, "But why again did we want to go home, Paul? It was really your idea."

"Yours?" Vicky asked, disappointed.

Paul turned to Vicky and admitted his defeat. "Okay, girl, you win."

Vicky celebrated as if Ayrton Senna[6] had just won a major Grand Prix. Vítor got startled by her screaming and pushed a button by mistake. Then he popped his head out of the machine and asked the reason of the celebration.

"Guess who is *not* leaving now."

---

6 Brazil's most loved F1 racer. He was proud of flying the Brazilian flag, a very uncommon feeling for Brazilians. He died in 1993 on a sad Sunday, in a crash during a race. When Brazil won the soccer World Cup that year, it dedicated its victory to him.

"Oh, you guys decided to stay?"

"We will stay here for today. But you can send us back to May first tonight, right?" John asked.

"Right."

"So, guys, why don't we go to the mall? I could use a snack." Vicky suggested. "And you told your mom we already ate, you freak. Now we can't even ask her for money."

"How do we go anywhere now, Vicky? My mom is home."

"Well, go upstairs, grab a bunch of books, and say that we're going to study down here."

"That's not a bad idea."

"And grab some cash out of your allowance while you're at it."

"What?"

"What, freak? I'll pay you back. Have I ever not?"

"Argh, okay, okay."

And so he did. And when he came back downstairs, he also had the keys to his parents' Elba[7]. "Do any of you guys drive?"

George volunteered.

---

7 A station wagon by Fiat, one of the most popular car companies in Brazil.

13 Soteropolitans And Liverpudlians

The whole gang hopped inside the Elba and headed to Shopping Barra Mall for a taste of 1993's fashion and technology. The first thing they all saw as they left Vítor's building was the McDonald's the children had referred to. That part of town, the children explained, was the Rio Vermelho neighborhood, part of the wonder-filled city of Salvador, Bahia.

"Wonder-filled until it rains." Vicky clarified.

"Then it's water-filled," Vítor added.

At the mall, the first stop was the food court. Everyone was ready for a snack. Besides, John, George, Ringo, and Paul still had a hard time believing they were really in the future. They had tons of questions. Questions that were better answered around a table filled with junk food. Vicky suggested they got some food at Pão de Batata, which was a sandwich restaurant like McDonald's, but authentically Brazilian.

John and Paul kept asking details about how that time machine, which had made them travel so many years in ten minutes, really worked. Vítor, proud of his invention, tried to explain some of Einstein's space-time relativity theory. "Well, he proved, at least in theory, that if we reached the speed of light, we could go forward in time for just a few seconds. If we multiply this speed by several trillions, we can go forward as much as we want, without, of course, getting any older. All we need is the right amount of energy for reaching that kind of speed."

"And how do you get that kind of energy?" John inquired.

Vítor stopped, smiled, and replied, "Top secret. It's nothing too complicated, but I doubt anyone else could think of it."

"Well, Vicky will tell us if Paul asks," John insisted.

"Hey," Vicky protested, "how do I know what this cuckoo kid is talking about? Vítor is kind of crazy."

"Come on, Vítor, tell us."

"Forget it, John, he won't even tell me."

"It's a very well-kept secret. The day the rest of the world finds it out, they will realize how stupid they have been for not having thought of it before."

"And you, smarty-pants, won't tell anyone."

"No, Ringo, it dies with me."

"You could make a lot of money with that, y'know?" Paul remarked.

"That's okay. I don't care."

"He's thirteen, Paul," John reminded him. "He doesn't care about money."

Paul shook his head smiling and went back to the logic of the trip, "So, we went forward in time. That makes sense. But Vicky traveled backwards. She went from ninety-three to sixty-four. How can you go back in time?"

"And we went back to the beginning of the first millennium," Ringo added.

"Yeah. How's that possible?"

"Oh, that's easy!" Vítor explained. "And of course, that was the whole point of Magic Vítor—regressing in time. We don't really want to know about the future. Right, Vicky?"

"Han? … oh, yeah," Vicky replied while carefully sneaking Paul's french fries from his tray to hers.

Paul saw that, looked at her funny, and pulled his fries back to his own tray. Vicky pretended nothing had happened and proceeded to pull Ringo's fries off his tray.

Paul saw that again and asked in confusion, "Vicky, are you still hungry?"

Vítor laughed and offered an explanation, "Vicky and I have this competition to see who's sneakier. She's not as good as I am," and showed them his tray.

They all looked at Vítor's tray. On it he had John's and George's fries and a few other things that did not belong to him.

The guys looked at him in amazement, and Vicky whispered to Paul, "I can steal kisses better than he can."

"Right. We know that," Paul replied, whispering as well, hoping John and Vítor had not heard that.

"What have we here? Bonnie and Clyde!" said John.

"Okay, how do you go back in time?" Ringo asked. He didn't care about the stealing competition as much as the time traveling explanation.

Vítor went on, still chuckling, "In order to do that, we just have to make the machine spin in negative speed. Remember that speed is a vectorized value. So we can direct it whichever way we want it."

"Come on, mate." John wouldn't let go. "Won't you tell us about the source of energy of this Magic Vítor?"

"Don't hold your breath for it, John," Vítor replied. "But I have another riddle for you, the simultaneous translation. You guys are British, and we are Brazilian. However ... are we speaking the same language?"

"Whoa! You got me there. Aren't we?"

"A-ha! We think we are. Each of us is actually speaking and understanding his own language. Thanks to the simultaneous translation."

"Oh, that's right. We are in Brazil," Ringo observed.

"But then, how is it possible?" John asked.

"Well, you know, I would not waste my time studying every language around. So I just bought a bunch of language books and bilingual dictionaries of all sorts of languages, put all those books inside the machine, and she does the rest."

"But you did program it to do that." Paul added.

"Of course," Vítor confirmed. "But that was easy."

"Easy? Speak for yourself, kid." Then he figured, "Oh. Vicky, that's why you don't have an accent."

"Oh yeah! You're right."

"Oh boy! Everything is just so simple! I never thought in

nineteen ninety-three people would have their own computers and could time travel," John marveled.

"And they can't."

"Say that again?"

"The time machine is exclusive. It's my creation."

John's voice got down to a whisper immediately, as if everyone could hear them. "You mean this is the only time machine in the whole world?"

"Oh yes."

The four guys looked at each other. Vítor made everyone's tension break into laughter with this added piece of information: "Imagine if there were other time machines. We'd have a time traffic jam!"

"Then who else knows about that?" George asked.

"No one else."

"If no one else knows about it, how did that wacky Gilmar end up in '64 then?" George went on.

"Oh, that? Edu told him."

"Well, then Edu knows it. And Edu is…?"

"A friend of mine."

"A mate of yours?"

"No. Actually, he is not exactly what I'd call a friend."

"So he is not even really your mate."

"Mate, do you realize what is going on here? You have the only time machine in the world, and you just go around telling anyone about it? Don't you think about how bad this can be? Oh, actually, just remember what happened yesterday…yesterday?" said John.

"That's right, John," Vicky said. "Yesterday."

Vítor thought about what he'd heard. He was definitely being reprimanded.

Paul tried to make it sound not so bad. "Look, Vítor, the time machine is really a great invention. Mate, you beat the time barrier, and two boys can be best friends, even if one of them is the other's grandfather. This is brilliant."

"Yes," John continued, "but let it fall on bad hands like

yesterday, and you might have a catastrophe in human history. You get it?

"Yeah, as in, don't leave that thing with Vicky, mate!"

"Wha-da-wa?"

George and John laughed at Ringo's joke and at Vicky's reaction, while Paul tried to remain serious and give him the "et tu, Brutus" look. Vítor, however, went livid as if he had been caught red-handed doing something naughty.

"Well, I … I have seen movies about it. I know that we must be careful not to alter the history continuum." Vítor thought for a moment and said, "You are right, John. I made a machine so perfect that anyone could …" Again he was silent for almost a minute and then went on, "You know what, as soon as you guys are back to your time, I will destroy the stupid machine."

The idea caused general discontentment. John claimed that was not his point. But Vicky was not just discontent; she was furious.

"John, see what you've done? Vítor, destroy it? You mean no more time traveling?"

"Darn, Vicky, I guess it's the right thing to do. What do you want me to do? Think of what John has said."

"Again, I did not mean that—"

"Look, gang," Vítor went on. "Time traveling? This is not a joke. Let's be reasonable and admit that we should not do it whenever we feel like it."

Vítor was not saying that just because. He was really under the impression he had done something bad, something really bad, just a few minutes ago back at home.

Vicky's stormy mood, however, had settled in. "All right! Forget about it! Never mind! I'll survive!"

No, it was not only Vicky. No one liked Vítor's idea. But didn't he claim to be the all-mighty machine owner who could decide everything about it? He was not changing his mind, even under Vicky's famous threats.

Ringo, however, had no trouble finding a way to get everyone's mind off that subject. "Hey, okay, let's forget about that. Since we are here, why don't we just enjoy the future? As you suggested, Vicky."

Ringo had hoped that suggestion would change Vicky's mood. He was right. She figured it was all or nothing from then on, and she'd rather have fun with the few hours she had left than to sit there and sulk. And Paul was still there, so all bets were off.

"Good idea. Let's walk around the mall. Maybe catch a movie."

"No, Vicky. Heck with movie." Vítor said.

"But it's *Jurassic Park*!"

"I don't got no money for movie tickets. Besides, this movie is so overrated. Let's take them to see our city. Maybe grab an ice cream at the Lighthouse."

"Oh, then let's go to the Abaeté Lagoon. This way we will also drive by the shoreline. On the way back, we can go see the sunset at the Lighthouse and get that icecream."

"Now you're talking. Is George up for the drive?"

"Fine with me. I enjoy driving."

"Okay, guys," Vicky explained, "we're going to see one of the tourist places of the coolest and most amazing cities of the whole entire world!"

"Until it rains!" they all repeated.

"You got it."

During the trip, they drove by the famous Salvador shoreline. There were many different beaches from the Barra Mall to the Abaeté Lagoon. Each beach had its own name. As they drove by each of them, Vicky told stories she had learned in third grade that explained how the beaches got their names. Most of the stories were made up, but they were fun to hear.

The Abaeté Lagoon is the famous "dark-water lake surrounded by white sand". A must-see to anyone who visits Salvador. Vicky's nickname for the white sand was Bahia snow, even though she had never seen snow in her life.

"Right on," Paul told her. "It looks exactly like snow. Just much hotter."

"I wish I could see real snow," she said.

After that, they still had time to drive all the way to Forte Beach to check out the Tamar Project, the one that takes care of sea turtles. And as the afternoon came to an end, they made their way back, as Vicky had suggested, to watch the sunset at the Barra Lighthouse. They sat a couple hundred yards away, on the wall next to the Christ Statue, which gave them a privileged view of the lighthouse—the most beautiful sunset in Salvador.

Since Vítor had previously suggested that they got ice cream at the Lighthouse, when Vicky saw the Kibon guy pushing his cart, she waved him over. They all got popsicles and sat on the wall facing the Lighthouse.

"Kibon ice cream at Barra Lighthouse. You can't get any more Soteropolitan[8] than this!" Vicky said.

8From Soteropolis - Greek for "the City of the Savior." Sotero – savior (Salvador in Portuguese); polis – city.

"Sotero-what?" John asked.

"Soteropolitan. That's what you call a native from the city of Salvador." But Vicky still had this little question in the back of her mind. So she asked Paul, "Paul, why did you want to leave so soon?"

"Why?"

"Yeah, why? Were you scared or something?"

"No, it wasn't that. Why did you never tell me that in ninety-three I will be married?"

"I didn't tell you?"

"Only when I got here. Why did you not tell me that before?"

"Ay, Paul, you did not know I came from the future."

"Then why did you go to sixty-four?"

"Because I wanted to meet you guys. Paul, John, George, and Ringo—you guys are my favorite stars ever. I am a Beatles fan, just like any other one in nineteen sixty-four."

"No. Like any other one, you're definitely not. But what I mean is, you know what you did. Why did you do it if you knew I was married?"

"Ay, did you know you'll beat the record of whys per minute?"

Paul smiled. But he kept on waiting for an answer.

Vicky explained, "Paul, girls are like that, okay? My mom's dream when she was a kid in the sixties was to marry Roberto Carlos. In the sixties this was very common among Brazilian little girls. Roberto was to Brazil as the Beatles were to the rest of the world. But see, my dream, even growing up in the nineties, has always been to hop into a time machine to get married to you. You know, girls do have these dreams. Even if we know they won't come true."

Paul had to laugh at that.

Vicky went on, "Yes, I know this is funny. But I do hope you'll understand."

"This is madness, Vicky!"

"Is that what you think? Well, never mind. See, how would I ever guess I'd really have a time machine? And how could I ever pass on chance of actually taking advantage of it? I had to try, you know."

He kept looking at her, shaking his head. "But you haven't even been born yet."

Vicky felt her heart sink. So that was what it was all about?

Paul, still chuckling, stated, "As I said, you're not like any other Beatles fan."

She smiled at the sound of that sentence. It sounded good to her. Then she looked back at the horizon. "Isn't the sunset from our Lighthouse really the most beautiful thing you've ever seen?"

"It certainly is."

"How can anyone live life without seeing this? I'm glad we brought you guys here."

She said that and watched it silently for a while. And so did Paul. But that conversation made him wonder. "Do I…do I love my…uh…wife? Do we love each other?"

"Are you going to be mad at me?"

Paul smiled at the way Vicky turned herself in. "I think I already know the answer to my question."

Vicky sighed and answered his question. "I think you guys are so happy together. Oh my gosh, you love her. And she loves you."

"And yet you came after me."

"Well, you see, I just figured that…if I got to you first…you would not miss her."

Paul looked at Vicky as if trying to figure out her argument.

"It does not make sense, I know," she apologized.

"Hmm… Actually, it does. But then what happens to Vítor's continuum theory?"

"Don't know, don't care."

Again Paul looked at Vicky, trying to figure her out. But really, now she had done it; she had gotten him curious about things.

"So, have I…have I not met her yet? The lady I'm going to—"

"Paul, stop it! Do you really want to know all of that?"

"Uh, yes."

"I don't know!"

"Yes, you do. You're the Beatles expert."

"Well, maybe I do, and I just don't want to tell you. And you can't make me, *mate*."

14 *Stop At That Pay Phone!*

Vítor had acted extraordinarily worried throughout the trip. Vicky had noticed that, and on the way back home, she asked him, "What is the matter with you, Vitty? The whole afternoon you seemed weird, as if things were not going well."

"Vicky, I am worried," he revealed in a secretive tone.

"Coming from you, this is no big news. But you're looking more worried than usual. What is the matter?"

"Do you remember when I was setting the machine to send your friends back to their time?"

"Uh-hmm."

"When you yelled, I got startled. And I think I pushed a button that I should not have."

"*Sweetie pea*, what's that supposed to mean?" She was beginning to worry too.

"I think I brought Gilmar back."

That revelation shocked Vicky. She had had it with Gilmar and did not want any more trouble with him. She had really hoped he had gotten stuck in sixty-four.

"You're messing with me."

"No, I am serious. I think Gilmar is here in ninety-three."

Ringo overheard this last line.

"What are you chaps saying? Gilmar came back to ninety-three?"

"I...am not sure. Maybe yes, maybe no."

"Paul won't like to hear that."

Paul had his face at the window, enjoying the trip, but as he saw Ringo, Vicky, and Vítor talking, he turned his head just in time to hear his name.

"I won't like what?"

"Gilmar is back here in ninety-three," Vicky revealed.

"Come again?"

"I am not sure. But I think I did something wrong when I was setting up the machine for you guys to go home. Then that was it, the machine started a countdown to bring him back. He might be at home waiting for us or up to something else."

When Vicky heard these words, a bad idea came to her mind.

"Vítor! Your mom!"

Vítor froze. "You think he'd dare?"

"Don't doubt it."

Vítor yelled to George, "Stop the car next to that pay phone!"

They were almost in front of the Ondina Apart Hotel. George pulled over and asked why.

"I've got to call home," Vítor yelled. And to Vicky, he said, "Do you have a token on you, Vicky?"

"Ever seen me carry tokens? Call collect."

"Argh, I'm not supposed to. But I will."

Vicky and Ringo stepped out of the car, and Vítor ran to the phone. There was already one person using it.

Meanwhile, Ringo explained to John and George, who had been chatting in the front seat, "He's calling home. It seems like our friend Gilmar is back here in ninety-three. He's afraid for his mom."

"But how?" George was confused.

John figured it all out. He stuck his head out the driver's window and called out to Vítor, "That's why you were so determined to destroy the machine, isn't it?"

Vítor nodded, embarrassed, confirming John's suspicion.

"Mate, after what we did to him, he will want revenge," George commented. "Now what do we do?"

"Wait, wait, wait! What are you chaps talking about? I am the one who should want revenge in this whole story. Man, I am the one who got punched for no reason. You'd better bet if I get my hands on that bloke..." Paul said that and did Vicky's fist-punching-hand thing. She looked at him, and they both laughed.

None of the other guys understood that reaction. Paul was

never the fighting kind of guy. They started joking, hoping he'd offer an explanation.

"It's the time travel, mate. It does things to your brain," Ringo joked.

"That's not the same bloke I met back in fifty-seven, eh." John joined in.

"No, I mean, you all saw what he did. You all know what he's done before. He'd better not try to mess with any of us again, or he'll have to deal with me."

Vicky enjoyed the idea very much and praised it. "My hero! My hero!"

"Yeah, little girl, just you'd better not cheer for him to punch me again."

"Ay, Paul, that was a joke!"

"But what have you guys done to the dude?"

Vítor was still not aware of the story that had happened in sixty-four. Vicky and the guys made a point of explaining it to him. By the end of the story, Vítor was really worried.

"Vicky, you'll never leave this guy alone, eh!" And to the guys, he said, "You guys have no idea what this girl has done to this man in the past."

"Was I alone, Vítor?"

"Well, I did too, but it was all your idea, remember? The plan came from your head."

"Which one?"

"The puke."

"Oh. Yeah."

"The puke?" John repeated.

Vicky smiled in pleasure. "Never mind."

"Vicky," Ringo said, "no wonder he came all the way to sixty-four after you."

"He lost his job because of her." John emphasized. "Really no wonder!"

Vítor had been waiting in line for the phone for about five minutes by then. So Vicky decided to say as loud as possible, "Some people just don't realize that pay phones are public, right,

Vitty!"

The guy on the phone did not take ten seconds to hang up after he heard that. He slammed the phone back on the hook and walked away. Vicky and Vítor thanked God for that, and he dialed home.

"No one answers."

"Try again."

He tried again. No answer. As he hung up again, very much worried, he glanced toward the bus stop across the street.

"Hey, isn't that Leo?"

"My brother? Where?"

"Shoot! Crossing the street. Coming toward us."

"Shoot! Ringo, get back in the car. Let's go, Vítor, before he sees us."

"No, too late. Okay, listen. This is a good thing. Get him to come with us. Get him to come with us. He might be able to help."

"Vítor, chillax. It's only one guy we're talking about."

"Yeah, and it's my mom we're talking about."

"Small Brains and her faggot friend! Whassup! " Leo greeted.

Leo was Vicky's little brother. He and Vítor were in the same grade and were always exchanging "niceties" disguised as swear words, a practice apparently related to boys' genetic make.

"What's up, momma's boy? Did Mommy allow Little Baby to go out on his own? Did she send your bottle?" Vítor greeted.

"No, fag, but she sent you a baby meal. Hey! What's my sister

98

doing in a car with a bunch of dudes? You two were supposed to be studying for the exams."

"Leo," Vicky said, "are you ready for an adventure?"

"I'm ready to hop on the bus with a hot girl from school. See her over there at the bus stop?"

"Well, wave bye-bye, and I will introduce you to the weird-looking dudes in the car. But you have to promise not to tell anyone."

"The heck! I'm telling."

"Promise, please. You won't regret it."

"Darn! Fine."

"Okay, because I am only doing that because I know you love Ringo Starr very much."

Vítor got impatient. "Vicky, do this or don't do it! We've got to get to my mom!"

"Leo, these guys here in the car are the Beatles, straight out of nineteen sixty-four."

Leo halted, perplexed. Then his face turned into a silly smile, and he asked, "What prank is this?"

"Do you like that idea? Now, what about this, I traveled to AD twenty-eight, and I saw Jesus!"

"You saw Jesus? Live?"

"Yes, old man, very quickly, but I sure did!"

"She's serious," Ringo helped. "I was there too."

"Vicky, you freak, is this for real?"

"Hey, idiot! Don't you see you're talking to Ringo Starr? Don't you see Paul, George, and John? What other proof do you need?"

"Hey, let's check with which one of us he looks like." John joked.

Leo started laughing because he was beginning to believe the craziest thing he could ever imagine.

"So you're Ringo Starr? I've always wanted to meet you!"

"Oh, Johnny, he looks like Ringo," Vicky said.

"Yeah, no one looks like me."[9]

"You're unique, Johnny." Paul remarked.

"Well, but your sister is not introducing you to Ringo Starr just because she loves you," said John.

"Of course not. I know my sister too well. What do you guys want?"

"First, you are not telling on us. Second, you're coming with us to help solve a problem."

The whole Gilmar story was explained to Leo, all the way from the beginning till the point in which they were considering the possibility that he had returned to nineteen ninety-three and might be a threat Vítor's mom.

"Dude, y'guys gotta problem, eh. So what? See that chick 'cross the street? Oh, I mean, crossing the street coming our way?"

Vítor panicked. He pushed Leo inside the car and got in as well. "Dude! You're coming with us *now*. Your girlfriend is one too many. Too bad for you that you decided to come talk to us." And to George, he commanded, "Step on it!"

"But Aline! Darn it! You faggot! Now she'll think I stood her up. What am I going to say? My sister and the *Beatles* needed my help?"

"Leo," Ringo said, trying to make peace, "since you *are* here, help us think up what to do with that bloke, will ya?"

"Duh, y'guys have a time machine, why don't you just send him somewhere he can't leave? I say send him to Nagasaki, nineteen forty-five."

"Hmm, good idea," Vicky agreed.

"Vicky, you're evil." John reprimanded her. But he could not help laughing.

She agreed with an evil smile, and her brother wasted no time. "She learned it from me. She learned it from me."

Everyone laughed at the children's sadism, but no one took their crazy idea seriously. And Vítor made sure he told them. "Guys, look, it's insane trying to send him anywhere in time

---

9 It turns out the guy who looks like John Lennon is the guy I married.

because we can never know what he will be up to anywhere. Had he stayed in sixty-four, wouldn't he try something to you guys?"

"Yes, but if you send him to, say, the Soviet Union in the year two thousand and stop the translation, it will be a while before he even knows what is going on and finds himself in the position to harm anyone." Interesting thought that one Ringo had, but one detail made the kids laugh. "What? You cannot stop the translation?"

"We can, Ringo, but you forgot to stop the Soviet Union, which is no more. Today it is only Russia, and maybe it will still be in the year two thousand," Vicky explained.

"Oh. Really?"

"Yeah, the Cold War is over and socialism lost."

Then Leo felt like showing off since Ringo himself was sitting right there. "Gang, before we decide what to do, why don't we find out if he is really here? I'm actually a pretty good strategist. I can help you guys make a plan to nail this guy."

15 *Fight! Fight! Fight!*

It was about seven-thirty p.m. when they all arrived at Vítor's home. And at half past seven in Salvador, it is always pitch-black outside. George parked the Elba across the street from the building, and they all hopped out quietly. Leo said that Vítor, Vicky, and himself should go ahead and see what they would find while the others should stay in the car checking for any strange movement, keeping the kids' backs. Then he said to Paul and his friends, "If you see anyone coming after us—"

"We run away," Paul joked. "It was a pleasure meeting you, mate."

"Freak."

"Don't you worry about a thing, Leo. We'll not let anything happen to you guys. We got your back."

Leo nodded and turned to Vítor. "Is that the time machine?"

Vítor nodded, and Leo showed which direction each one of them should follow; he would check inside the machine, Vicky should go through the parking lot, and Vítor should go up the stairs to his condo.

*

Leo opened the door carefully. He did not understand anything at all. He looked back at the rest of the people and again inside of the machine. There, unconscious, thrown against the wall, bound and gagged, lay a little boy. It was Joshua, the boy Vicky had met in Judea. Right away he realized they were not alone.

*

Vítor lived on the third and last floor of the small building. He was already on the second flight of stairs when he saw Edu coming down from his condo, carrying food and a cold one-liter Coca-Cola bottle.

"Edu? What are you doing in my home?"

Edu did not think twice. He dropped everything on the floor and threw the Coca-Cola bottle at Vítor. The bottle hit him in the head and made him fall down the stairs. Edu did not wait for Vítor to get up; he jumped on him, kicking and punching. The two of them went rolling down the remainder of the stairs. Edu was much taller than Vítor, so he had an easier time controlling the fight.

Leo heard the noise and looked for his sister.

"Vicky?"

*

Vicky had entered the parking lot and was walking attentively among the cars and pillars when she heard the half-whispered call of her brother. She turned for a second to see what the matter was. And, in that second, she was surprised by Gilmar, who held her from behind. With the tip of his pocketknife against her chin, he threatened her in a whisper, "Say a peep and you're done, Vicky."

As Leo heard no word from his sister, he became even more apprehensive. He looked at the place where the noise had come from and saw Vítor and Edu rolling down the stairs all the way to the ground floor.

At this point, he saw no reason to watch how loud his voice was. There was no more need to be sneaky. He yelled to the others, "Gang, Gilmar really is here! I'm going to need help! Paul, Vicky is over there in the parking lot! Run over there!" Then he ran to help out Vítor.

Paul had needed no warning though. From where he was he

could hear the noise too and looked to check on Vicky. At the moment Leo yelled to him, he had just seen her. He had also seen that Gilmar was holding her.

"Ringo, look! Over there."

"I'll run toward them to distract him while you grab him from behind."

Paul and Ringo immediately followed through with that plan.

John noticed Vítor fighting the other kid by the stairway.

"George, come with me," he said, and they both ran across the street toward the building.

When Gilmar realized he had been found, he moved away from behind the pillar to where everyone could see him.

"You stop right there or the girl dies!" he yelled to Ringo.

Ringo had no choice. He did not want to fool around with a guy holding a blade to Vicky's throat. John and George slowed down too, and tried to sneak by to get to where Vítor was. Paul hadn't been seen yet, so he kept creeping through the cars.

"What's up with you, Gilmar? Why do you need me? If you really want to kill me, why haven't you already?" Vicky asked.

"Because you deserve something worse than that, idiot! Because, in case you don't remember, I have a personal issue with you. And now that I have the time machine under my control, I can teach you not to mess with me. I had another hostage to trade for you, some Joshua kid, but you made things easier."

"Joshua? You jerk! What did you do to him?"

Gilmar yelled to everyone else, "Now I am going in the machine with Vicky. If no one moves, I might leave her alive somewhere in time. But you try anything funny, and this blade will cut her neck."

"You don't mean that," Vicky challenged him.

"Try me."

As soon as he uttered these words, Paul surprised him from behind, jumping on him from the roof of a car. Vicky screamed, set herself loose, ran to the machine, and closed the hatch.

Paul and Gilmar were left behind fighting for the direction of the blade.

Meanwhile, Leo and Vítor had just immobilized Edu. Each of them held one of his arms down. That's when John and George got to them.

George used his shirt to tie Edu's arms behind his back and said to Vítor, "Let's go up to the flat to check on your mum."

Vítor obeyed, leaving Edu under Leo and John's watch.

"Leo, keep an eye on him. I'm going to go find your sister."

Inside the machine, Vicky tried to wake Joshua up. But she found a Swiss pocketknife in the midst of Edu's possessions. She grabbed it and slipped it into her pocket.

Suddenly, the hatch opened again. It was John. "How are you, girl?"

"Good. Where's Paul?"

"He and Ringo are taking care of your nutty professor. And there's another bloke over there, but Leo and Vítor took care of him. He's obviously a mate of your teacher's. What's up with this little lad? How on Earth did he get here?"

"I don't know. Somehow Gilmar found him. I hope he is all right. If Gilmar did something to him…"

*

Vítor and George found Cláudia lying on the laundry room floor, bound and gagged. They ran to untie her.

"Mom, you all right?"

"Two criminals break into my house, beat me, tie me up, throw me on the floor of the laundry room, take the food I have in the house, and you're asking me if I'm all right?"

"Calm down, Mom." Vítor said, holding her shoulders and looking into her eyes. "We are here now. Everything will be fine."

She sighed, trying to calm herself down.

"That's all right, baby boy. Thank you."

*

It seemed as if Paul just couldn't ever win when it came to fighting Gilmar. Even when Ringo was already holding Gilmar's right arm, he was still able to knee and punch Paul on the nose, leaving him on the ground.

Ringo tried to take revenge. He hit Gilmar right on his stomach and, pushing his wrist against a pillar, forced the knife to fall in his hand. "I'll take care of this for you."

However, he lost control of Gilmar when he tried to put away the pocketknife. Gilmar twisted Ringo's wrist, pushed him against a pillar and ran toward the machine. John saw that and, leaving Vicky with Joshua, ran to try to stop him. But Gilmar was coming so fast and so desperately that he knocked John down on the way.

As Vicky noticed that Gilmar was coming toward her, she closed the hatch, buckled Joshua, and tried to program the machine. Ringo, John, and Leo ran after Gilmar, but he was just fast enough to open the hatch and walk in before the machine got started. When the others got there, it was too late.

As for Paul, he watched the whole scene lying on the ground with a bleeding nose. He hid his head in his hands, and John yelled at him, "Bloody hell, Paul! Can't you ever win a bloody fight?"

"Where's Vicky?" George asked as he and Vítor arrived, followed by Cláudia.

"Vicky, Joshua, and Gilmar disappeared with the machine." replied John.

"So what do we do now?"

Leo knew exactly what to do. Didn't Gilmar take his sister without him being able to do anything about it? So he'd take it out on his brown-nose number one. He ran toward Edu and kicked him as hard as he could. "You idiot!"

"What do we do now?" Paul, disappointed, repeated George's question.

Vítor watched Paul with mixed feelings of anger and pity.

16 The 1500's And The 1500's

~~~~~~~~~~~~~~~~   ~~~~~~~~~~~~~~~~

The machine was coming to a stop. Inside, Joshua was beginning to wake up.

"Where are we?" Gilmar yelled at Vicky.

"I have no idea. I was trying to run away from you. I did not pay attention to what I was doing."

"Darn! This does not matter. Hop out! The trip for the two of you ends here."

"What?"

Joshua looked up and recognized the historical scene he had been hearing about from babyhood.

"I know this! It's the exodus from Egypt. We are in the middle of the Red Sea! Look!"

Vicky and Gilmar looked outside. It was a scary scene! There was a huge wall of water on each side, and right ahead they could see the Egyptian army charging toward them.

Gilmar froze. Vicky felt her stomach twist. But she remembered that while the Jewish people were in there, the waters would remain parted.

"Where's Moses with the Jewish people?"

"There they are! Almost done crossing the sea! Vicky, this whole wall of water will come down on us!"

"Oh no, it won't!"

As fast as possible, Vicky went and changed the letters BC to AD and turned the key. The machine had barely reached the right speed when the waters came down with a roar.

~~~~~~~~~~~~~~~ ~~~~~~~~~~~~~~~

"Where the hell are we right now, you brat?" Gilmar yelled.

"How am I to know? When did the Exodus happen? We are on the equivalent date on the AD era."

Vicky and Gilmar looked outside. There was a good amount of Tupi-Guarani Indians and a few white people dressed in pompous European clothes.

"I can't believe it! This is Brazil! It must be the year 1500. We are watching the discovery of Brazil!"

"Great for me. Awful for you two. I am making a stop here to watch this episode, then I will decide where to go next. You guys have reached your final destination."

"Ha! No way, professor!"

"Ha! Yes way!" he said and punched her.

The girl saw everything go black.

*

When Vicky came to, she noticed her hands were tied, and

she saw Gilmar still tying her feet. Joshua, who still had hands and feet tied, was lying right next to her. Gilmar had dragged them into the forest to a place removed from where the other people were, but from where they could still see everyone.

"You two will stay right here, nice and quiet. If the Indians are good to you, they might let you go. But they might also think you're enemies or some kind of cursed children. That will be fun to watch. Too bad I will not be here for that."

"You-you creep! When Paul gets you—"

"Who? That wimp? I have taken care of him twice, and I can take care of him permanently if you want me to. I have a time machine. He doesn't even get to be born if I don't want him to."

"Are you insane? The time machine was built because of him. If anything happens to him or to his parents, there will never be a time machine. You're not going to lay as much as a finger on him."

"Oh, Vicky, that's cute. What are you going to do about that?"

She looked at him, mad, not knowing what to say.

"Listen, stupid little girl, I don't care about your darling Paul McCartney. As long as he doesn't stay in my way, I could care less what happens to him. All I wanted was to get rid of you and to get the machine so I can use it for bigger and better plans."

"Plans? What plans?"

"Getting to know past, present, and future might be very lucrative. Visionaries always have the world at their feet. So as long as your friends don't cause me any trouble, I will leave them alone. Unfortunately for you, that option no longer exists."

"You freak!" She spat in his face.

Gilmar wiped his face and gave a triumphant smile. "What goes around comes around. Who would have thought that the same person who ruined my life would provide me with the tools for world domination?" Having said that, Gilmar stood up and left them.

"Jerk! You will regret that! You hear me? You'll pay for that!"

Gilmar did not bother looking back. He just walked away,

smiling and shaking his head.

Joshua and Vicky watched him go. She looked down, annoyed, thinking up a way out of that situation. Joshua watched her.

"Vicky, I'm scared. Who are these Indians?"

Vicky sighed, let her head fall back on the tree, and said, trying not to cry, "My ancestors. This whole thing is like a nightmare."

"What will we do, Vicky? We can't let him leave without us."

"What we *can't* do is leave here *with* him. We have to run away and leave him trapped here."

"But how?"

"Can you put your hand inside my pocket and pull a

pocketknife from there?"

"Inside your what? To pull a what?"

"You don't know these words. Look, this here is my pocket. Can you put your hand in there and pull out anything you find?"

"I think I can try."

Try he did, and he found what she wanted. He pulled the knife she had grabbed from Edu's possessions out of her pocket.

"Well done, Joshua! This thing you're holding is a Swiss pocketknife. Expensive little guy. Not everyone can afford it. It's got an array of—"

Joshua watched her with a lost look in his eyes, not knowing whether to pay any attention or to tell her to hurry. But simply by looking at the boy's little face, she figured as much.

"We can talk about this later. Let's set ourselves free. Hand it to me."

She opened the knife and, with a little hard work, cut the rope that tied the boy's hands.

"I'm free."

"Now, careful not to hurt me. Cut the rope off of my hands."

"All right."

Joshua took the knife and cut the rope that tied the girl's hands.

"Good job, kiddo!"

Now that their hands were free, it was easy for them to untie their feet.

"That's it, we're free. Now let's get out of here real quick, back to nineteen ninety-three."

"What is that?"

"That's the number of the year we live. You live in the year twenty-eight Anno Domini, or AD. Vítor and I are from AD nineteen ninety-three, and those other guys are from AD nineteen sixty-four."

"Wow! You came from far, far away. What year is this now?"

"It must be AD fifteen hundred, the discovery of my country, Brazil."

"What about the Red Sea?"

"That's on the BC era—that means Before Christ. That's around fifteen hundred BC."

"So you guys in the future count the years according to the Christ's life? The Christ of the Jews? Is it Jesus?"

"That's right, that's him."

"Wow!"

Vicky smiled and rushed him, "But now we'd better go. We can talk better when we're in nineteen ninety-three." Suddenly she had an idea. "Actually, we should stop some other year before that. Let's go."

The two of them ran to the machine. From afar they could see Gilmar entertaining the Portuguese men.

"Look at him over there. Let's go have some fun."

"How?"

"Hey! Gilmar! Hey, freak!"

Gilmar looked and, calmly, drove his attention back to what he was doing. When he realized, however, what he had just seen and heard, he looked quickly back at the children's direction and ran toward them.

"You need to learn to tie ropes!"

"Vicky, let's go! He's coming our way! He runs faster than us! Let's go!"

"Let's go! Let's go! Quick! This time we can't afford mistakes!"

They charged toward the machine, this time for good. But Joshua fell halfway there.

Vicky only noticed it when he called out, "Vicky, wait up!"

She stopped to look and lost all the momentum. The time it took for her to go back, help the boy up, hold on to his hand, and run was enough for Gilmar to almost catch up with them.

"Run for your life, Tiny!"

They reached the machine with Gilmar close behind. They opened the hatch, Joshua got inside, and Vicky yelled for him to buckle. That was when Gilmar grabbed her.

This time she did not hesitate; she thrust the knife at his face, hopped in, and closed the hatch.

"Hold the door tight, Tiny! Don't let him open!" she said while punching in the right numbers.

Joshua held the hatch tight. He was not that strong at all, but his fear, as he watched the violence with which Gilmar banged the hatch, increased his strength about a million times.

The machine began to spin. Gilmar did not let go of it until it was gone. He was shot into the air and disappeared.

17 *Private Tutors Revised*

The roles had changed now. It was Edu who was bound and thrown on the floor.

"Tell us! Where were you guys going? Gilmar must have told you." Vítor screamed, grabbing the boy by the shirt's neck.

"I don't know, I swear! All he said was we were on our way to make lots of money. Something about inventions. And he kept talking about vengeance against Vicky and ... the Beatles?"

Vítor pushed Edu and got up, furious as a wild animal.

"Wait, Vítor. Maybe he really doesn't know." John tried to calm him down.

"Yes, but that is what I am scared of." Vítor answered.

Paul was sitting on the floor against a marble pillar. Cláudia had taken care of his nose, and now was sitting by his side.

"You guys are not tutors, are you?" she asked him.

"No. We're not."

"Can you tell me what on earth is going on?"

"Never mind. You won't believe it."

"I won't believe what?"

Paul did not want to answer that. Cláudia insisted. "I won't believe what?"

He sighed and shook his head. Then he turned to Cláudia and said, "My name is Paul McCartney. And this morning I woke up in nineteen sixty-four."

"What?"

"I told you you'd not believe it," he replied as if he really didn't care whether or not she believed him. Then he called out

117

to Vítor, "Can't you build another machine so we can go after them?"

Vítor looked at him with contempt. "Are you out of your mind, dude? Do you think it's easy to make one of these? Stay in your place, Paul."

"Vítor! Is that how I raise you?"

"Hey, Vítor, what's up with you? Do you have to talk to the guy like that? He was trying to offer a suggestion." Leo said.

"An idiot one if you did not notice, Leo," Vítor replied.

"Oh yeah, freak? But at least he said something. And you look like you're jealous."

"Jealous? Are you tripping, Leo?"

"Yes, jealous, poop face! Because Vicky always liked him and never liked you."

"You're such a retard, Leo! It has nothing to do with that. I am mad at this guy. It's so easy to talk! I wanted to have seen this faggot break Gilmar's face when he had the chance. He could not do that."

"Don't be stupid, Vítor."

"Hey, you two. Stop it, okay." Paul said back on his feet. "Listen here. If there's one thing I don't need is people to defend me. There's already too much going on for you lads to start a fight."

The boys, embarrassed, looked at each other and stopped arguing.

"I am sorry. I'm sorry," Vítor said, looking at the ground. And then he looked at John. "It's just that this feeling of not being able to do anything makes me mad."

"Makes you scared, you mean."

"I guess."

"We're all scared of what might happen, Vítor. But all we can do is hope that Vicky solves this problem. She has the machine. If she can find a way out, she'll certainly find her way back."

"You're right, John. But what if she doesn't? God knows in what time or place she ended up and what Gilmar will be up to. If they run out of fuel, she won't know what to do. Depending on the time period she's in, they won't even have the fuel the machine needs. Besides, you guys won't be able to go back to '64."

"Well, couldn't you—" Ringo was about to suggest the same thing Paul had, but for fear of causing more trouble, he stopped halfway through.

"Oh my gosh!" That was Cláudia. She had been lost in her thoughts, trying to figure out what was going on. Time traveling? That was science fiction! Her son, as smart as he was, could not make people travel in time. Or could he? She was having these thoughts while studying the face of each one of the guys, listening to every single word they said as if in a haze. Then she finally snapped out of it. "Oh my gosh! You really are Paul McCartney, aren't you?"

Paul made a face as one who says, *Wow, lady! It took you a while, eh.*

"And you are Ringo and John. And…George Harrison! Vítor! What am I going to do with you?"

"Let me live?"

She had no idea whether to feel angry or thrilled. So after looking at him with a half smile half frown, this was her reply: "Maybe. But I really hope Vicky's all right. Because I will be the one explaining to her mother why her daughter is not coming back home anymore."

" The problem is that most of the time my sister has not a clue what she does."

"What do you have against your sister?" Ringo asked.

"Nothing. I just don't think she knows how to handle trouble."

"She's handled it before, Leo."

Leo's only reply was a sad smile, and a question, "Does she even know what is this fuel?"

"No." Paul replied, staring at Vítor. "She was never told."

But they did not have to wait any longer. The machine appeared, followed by the lightning and wind they had seen before.

"They're here!" Ringo cheered.

"No, Ringo, wait! It might be Vicky, but it might also be Gilmar," John said.

"If it is Gilmar and if he is alone, we pound him to death first, then we ask questions."

They all placed themselves around the machine, waiting for it to stop spinning. They all did, except for Paul, who remained leaning against the pillar, not wanting to get any closer.

The machine stopped at last. A few seconds later the hatch slowly opened. Everyone was apprehensive. A smile of relief came when they saw Vicky and Joshua, still groggy, trying to get out.

"Where's Gilmar?" Vítor asked.

"Huh? Gilmar? Oh yes! It seems he stayed with Cabral, discovering Brazil in 1500.[10]"

Everyone celebrated, even those who had no idea who Cabral was.

"Cheers, Vicky!" Ringo said.

When she heard Ringo's words, Vicky tried walking out of the machine, but she was about to fall. She tried holding on to the machine as he ran to hold her.

"Careful there, young lass!"

10Pedro Álvares Cabral discovered Brazil in April 21, 1500.

"Yeah, I'm dizzy Miss Lizzy! Someone hold the kiddo over there, or he'll fall face-first on the marble floor."

Joshua began to get out of the machine, his feet unsure whether to step on the floor or on the moon. George ran for him.

Ringo stared at Vicky and asked in a whisper, "Are you sure Gilmar stayed in fifteen hundred? I mean, he is not making you say that, right?"

"Nah. He tried to get in at the time we were running away from him, but he didn't make it. We were stronger!"

Ringo wasted no time to prove Leo wrong. "I knew you would be able to rid yourself of that bloke. Your brother here didn't seem to think you'd be able to get back to us."

"My brother is jealous 'cause I'm smarter than he his. That's why he calls me Small Brains, don't you know that?"

"Ha! Look who's talking! If you don't spend the day with your head buried in a book, you can't event say the ABC by heart. Who gets A's without ever opening a book?"

"Shut up. At least I'm responsible."

"Vicky, tell him about the Red Sea," Joshua tried to help out his friend.

"Red Sea?" Ringo repeated.

Vicky looked at her brother with a triumphant smirk and explained, "We were in the middle of the Red Sea. You know, that story in the Bible that God opens up the sea for the Jews? We had to get out of there right away, because as soon as the Jews were gone the waters would close on us. I changed the letters from BC to AD, and turned on the machine. The thing sped up and disappeared right when the waters were coming down. The next moment we were in just-discovered Brazil. Beat that, little brother!"

Everyone was impressed by Vicky's story. But John still couldn't reconcile one small detail:

"What about the new clothes you two are wearing?"

"Oh, darling! You bought them for us!" Vicky said.

"I did?" John was confused.

Vicky and Joshua smiled a naughty smile. She went on, "We

went to visit you. Joshua and I took advantage of the fact that we had gotten rid of Gilmar and spent two days time touring."

"You took advantage of my machine, eh." Vítor said, "I wish the fuel had run out. Then what would you guys do?"

Vicky did not care to answer that. She figured she owed no more explanations. Now she was worried about only one thing, "Where's Paul?"

The others just looked at where Paul was. He was still just watching the scene. But standing next to him was ... ouch! Vicky gasped. "Aunt Cláudia!"

"Don't try to come up with excuses, Miss Vicky! Your boyfriend here already told me the whole story."

"Boyfriend? I never told you that I was her—"

"Oh, sweetheart, don't take offense. We all know that Vicky's got a crush on you. Some of us had to learn it the hard way."

Vicky felt her face burn. But she figured she would not find an excuse to explain Aunt Cláudia's remarks, so she went back to her original intention of complaining about the reception. Or lack of it. "Won't you come talk to me, Paul?"

It took him a while to reply to that, but he finally told her, while keeping his eyes on the ground, "I had the chance to stop Gilmar, and I couldn't. If he had done anything to you, it would have been all my fault." He looked back at her. "Do you still want to talk to me?"

"Ay, Paul, don't be a fool! What matters is that you took the risk to go after him to try to save me. I mean, okay, he took the best out of you, but so what? Didn't everything turn out just fine?"

"So you're not disappointed with me?" he asked, staring at her.

She replied, leaning against his pillar, "No, silly! It's your courage that made you my hero!"

These words gave him some motivation. He turned to look at Vicky with a timid smile. "Well, at least now you know I can't do *anything*."

"Ok, almost anything. Hug?"

Paul laughed at the little-kid voice she used and gave her a hug.

"So pretty much what happens is I'm the one who keeps getting her out of trouble and Paul is the one who keeps taking the credit for being the hero." Ringo mentioned to Leo.

"Ouch," Paul replied to that comment. "Someone is jealous."

"Ringo, do you want hug, too?" Vicky asked.

"Nah, I will let this be you guys' special moment." Ringo replied.

Then Vicky had an idea, "We could end the day with a trip to ITA."

Paul didn't get it. What on earth was ITA? Neither his friends nor Joshua knew it. However, Vítor, his mother, and Leo knew it very well. And the two boys loved the idea.

"Tonight? That's rad! Let's do it!" Leo said.

"But let's hurry. So we can go on every ride." Vítor agreed.

"Ain't that a sweet idea?" Vicky asked the two of them.

"Sweet!" they both replied.

However, Paul, who, just like the others, could not understand what they were talking about, asked, "Hey, mates, what are you talking about? What the heck is ITA?"

"The ITA is a super awesome amusement park with many new rides and a great advantage: you only pay to enter. Then you can go on any ride you want, as many times as you want."

A place where you only had to pay to enter and could go on any ride for free was an incredible novelty for any child growing up in Salvador.

The four guys looked at each other, and Ringo concluded, "It sure sounds like fun."

"Yeah, and whose pocket will you be picking to afford this extravaganza, Vicky?" Cláudia asked.

"Vítor's allowance. But I'll pay him back."

Vítor shook his head at her. "Forget it. My money ran out this afternoon, when we had ice cream at the lighthouse."

"Well, can't you ask your mom for an advance, then?"

The guys were dismayed when they heard Vicky say that.

"Whoa! What is that? We ain't making your mum spend money," John said.

"Vicky, how can you invite us to go to a park at other people's expenses?" Paul asked.

"Uh … I didn't think- I thought we had money. Vítor, you know I always pay you back. Tell them." Noticing the way the guys looked at her, she felt she had to go on. "I'm serious. I sell homemade candy and stuff at school, so I always have pocket money. I just didn't plan for this."

"Oh, come on," Cláudia said, almost complaining about their shyness. "That's okay. I will pay for you all."

"No, absolutely not," Paul persisted. "Don't you worry about us! We're not spending someone's hard-earned money to go have fun."

"Don't be silly! I don't have the Beatles dropping by every day. You won't deny me the honor of paying for you guys to go to the park."

"See! That's right! She makes a point." Vicky said.

"Girl, you are just too bold." Paul said.

"I am. You know I am," she said, smiling at him.

John laughed at Paul and thanked Cláudia in the name of his friends. "Well, if you insist, what can we do? Cheers!"

"That's right, Mr. Lennon." Then she turned to her son and said, "Vítor, come upstairs with me, help me find a shirt for George to wear. Come along, George."

Cláudia, Vítor, Leo, and George went upstairs.

"Vicky," Joshua asked "what is an amusement park?"

While Vicky was busy trying to explain to Joshua what an amusement park was, Paul, John, and Ringo conferred.

"We're not really letting Vítor's mum pay for our park tickets, are we, mates?" Paul whispered.

"No! Of course not!" John agreed. "We've got our own money! We've got way more money than they do. It's not fair that she pay for us."

"Then what? Because all of our cash is back in '64."

Ringo suggested, "Well, this is the future. Right? Get her

address, wait thirty years, mail her a check."

Paul and John stared at Ringo as if he had just invented the wheel.

"Ringo!"

"Did I just say something stupid again?"

"That's brilliant! You chaps wait for me down here," John said and climbed up the stairs, running.

*

George had just put on a button-up shirt that belonged to Vítor's dad and looked at himself in the mirror.

"Is that good?" Cláudia asked.

"It's my dad's," Vítor added. "He hardly ever wears it. Ugly, eh."

"Vítor!" Cláudia censored the boy. "Don't say that!"

"Oh, Mom," he said in a mocking tone, "you never had good taste on gifts for Dad." And to George, he said, "This is almost as old as I am. My dad might have worn it once or twice."

George smiled in embarrassment, looking at Cláudia. She sent Vítor a nasty look, opened the wardrobe, grabbed a brand new T-shirt, and threw it at George.

Leo showed up at the door. "Let's go, guys?"

"Let's!" Vítor yelled.

Cláudia grabbed the cash and put it in Vítor's hand.

"Here you go. Money for tickets and snacks."

"You not coming?"

"Honey, you kids are something, you know that? I will have to take care of the mess you left downstairs. I will call the police and turn that boy in for burglary. Now take your machine with you guys. It will be much easier to explain how the house was burglarized if there's no time machine to back up his story." She sighed. "You kids!"

"Oh, okay. Mom … thanks a lot." he said, feeling guilty. Then he turned to his friends. "Let's go, guys."

George and Leo said good-bye to Cláudia and went out the

door. Cláudia called her son back.

"When your friends are gone, however, we'll have a serious talk, young man."

Vítor swallowed.

"And let Vicky know that she will be talking to her mom as well."

Vítor swallowed again. However, he decided he would not tell Vicky anything. They were off to ITA, and she had her favorite stars along with her. It was like a dream. He'd not ruin that.

He started his way out and almost slammed into John, who had come out from hiding behind the door, thinking everyone had already gone down the stairs.

"What are you doing up here?"

"Hey, mate, got a toilet?"

"Oh, sure. We have one in the bathroom. Second door to the right. Meet you downstairs."

Vítor started his way downstairs wondering why John would have thought there would be a toilet behind the condo door. He had no idea toilet was just a way British people used to refer to a bathroom. When he got downstairs, he said to the rest of the group, "This time, for safety, we're going on the Magic Vítor."

"We can do that?" Paul asked.

"Sure. Same day, different place," said Vítor.

"Cool," Vicky said.

"It's just going to be a little teeny bit crowded in there. We have two extra people."

18 *Guaraná and Guava*

The park ticket was not expensive if you considered the things you could do there. After paying for the tickets, Vítor split the rest of the money equally among everyone so they could all get snacks.

The wild rides were the favorite among them.

Vicky's favorite was the Bamba, a giant disk with benches on the edge. You sit on them and hold on for dear life while the ride shakes you up and down, trying to throw you off it. No seat belts. Just your arms. Very unsafe! She used to get all sore the day after.

Joshua cried on the roller coaster, so he skipped the other wild rides. As any kid his age, he enjoyed the carousel, the choo-choo train, the bounce house, and he loved the candy apple that his friends got him into trying.

After a ride called the Typhoon, however, Vicky regretted having had a Brazilian hot dog11 while waiting in line. The Typhoon is a two-seater spaceship that is linked to an axis by a metal bar. It spins fast on the axis as it moves up and down. Not a good choice if you're prone to motion sickness as she was. As soon as they got in the line for the bumper cars she knew it was time to run away, far, far away from human beings to throw up the hot dog she had just devoured.

Well, nothing a five-minute walk around the park won't heal. But she wasn't about to spend those five minutes alone. She dragged Paul along with her.

11Brazilian hot dogs are more like sloppy joes—the hot dog is cooked with tomato sauce, onions, and peppers and served on a hot dog bun. If fully loaded, add ketchup, mustard, mayo, and Parmesan cheese.

"You really just pulled me away from the bumper cars line. You realize that, don't you?"

"I need company. Let's grab *Guaraná* [gwa-rah-*nah*] and a pastry."

"What's *Guaraná*?"

"Oh my gosh, old man! Brazil's favorite soda! It's a berry you can only find in the Amazon Rainforest. It's my favorite drink. You've got to try it. Let's do that?"

"Are you sure you want to eat or drink anything now? I mean, after you just-"

"Pretty sure. I need something mild to make me feel better. I'm still nauseous. That stupid ride. I'm never doing Typhoon again. It's like riding on a car. I get car sick a lot. But anyways, you need to try *Guaraná*. What d'you say?"

"Okay, sure."

They grabbed two drinks and two pastries with guava filling.

"Let me know if you like it. You will. Some people prefer Coke, but seriously? *Guaraná* is so much better. That's the kind of stuff my family and I argue over dinnertime."

They both giggled.

"Sounds like a good argument to have at dinner. Hey, this thing is really good!"

"Aunt Regina hates it. She only drinks Coca-Cola. You know something? She would love to be here."

"Aunt...Regina?"

"Yup. She loves rides just like me. Actually, all of my aunts would love to be here. They were all Beatles fans. Except for my mom and my Aunt Luana, who really liked Roberto Carlos. Their dream was to—"

"Marry me?" Paul risked, thinking that was funny.

"Oh, n-no. They... I don't know, really. There was Jerry Adriani, and there was Erasmo Carlos, and there was Roberto Carlos of course. Roberto is the King. The king of music. Because there's Pelé, who is the king of soccer. But, really, everyone loved Roberto. I think they all wanted to marry him. Except for me, of course. I wanted to—"

"Vicky!"

"Sorry. You don't want me to say that."

"No, that was not it. Just...how many words per second can you say?"

"Oh! A lot! I didn't used to talk at all. But then one day I began talking and never stopped again. But only when I am excited. Like now. Like, when I first met you guys, yesterday, I was scared, so I didn't talk much. Aunt Regina says I am a motor mouth. People keep telling me to be quiet."

"No wonder. You're talking like a machine gun. And, actually, yesterday you talked just as fast."

Vicky giggled. "You're telling me to be quiet, aren't you?"

"Uh, well, it's just that you're saying all those names of people

I don't know. Can you just slow down?"

"Well, since it's you that's asking … I guess I can."

After a few seconds in silence, Paul laughed. "I still can't believe this is really happening. When I agreed to get into that machine, I really thought that time-travel story was just a prank."

"Now you believe me?"

"Well, there's always the possibility that you put something really weird in my scrambled eggs this morning and this is all just a wild dream. Other than that, I guess I don't have a choice but to believe you."

"I hope you're having fun."

"I am, actually. I am glad you brought us here. Thank you."

"*Oxe*, you're welcome. I bet it's way more fun for me. I'm hanging out with Paul McCartney!"

"Yes, but I actually get to walk around like a regular human being. But anyway, you said you have an aunt named Regina. Isn't that your name too? You're Regina, too. Right?"

"Yeah, I don't like naming children after other people in the family, but my family likes to do that. It gets so confusing. People call the house and go like 'Can I talk to Regina?' and we go like, 'Which one?' That's why I just tell people to call me Vicky."

"Yeah, I know what you mean."

"We shouldn't do that to our children."

Our children? Oh, that did not sound like an innocent remark. Paul looked at her funny and switched subjects. "What about Aunt Cláudia? You and Vítor cousins?"

"Oh, Aunt Cláudia is not my real aunt. That's just what we call grownups in Brazil."

"That's right." He smiled. "She's your ex-future-mother-in-law."

Vicky looked down with a shy smile. "You crazy? Vítor and I are friends."

"He told me you two dated."

"... Yeah, ... but I did not really like him."

"I know that. He told me the whole story."

"Vítor did? Wow. But you don't really care."

Paul shook his head, smiling. "You're something, Vicky. … I think he still likes you, y'know."

Vicky's eyes kept watching the gravel, but her smile had disappeared.

"You think- you think I'm stupid?"

"What?"

Vicky gathered up the courage to stare Paul in the eyes and ask, "Be honest. Do you think I am stupid?"

Paul was surprised by that question. It took him a while to reply, but when he did, he was assertive. "No! Absolutely not, Vicky! Of course not!"

"So if … if I were to move to 1964, would you date me?"

"Ha! This conversation is going way too far, little girl. Look, Vicky, you're too young for me, don't you think?"

"Yes, but—"

He put his arm around her shoulders and said, "Let me tell you something. I think you're a very special girl. More than any other I have met. And I've met quite a few."

Vicky smiled as she recognized that line from one of her favorite Beatles songs. But her worries weren't gone. "Yes, but … special like how? Not like a girlfriend."

"No, come on. But I do really like you. Isn't that enough?"

Vicky felt her face burning once again. She looked at Paul and, very matter-of-fact, said, "No."

"We belong to different times. What can we do?"

"Will you change your mind if I go back in nine years? To sixty-four?"

Paul looked down for a moment. Then he looked back at her. "Vicky, no. Don't you even consider that. You're not waiting nine years for me. Besides, you're really thirty-eight years younger than me. You realize that, right?"

Vicky looked away and did not answer that. She looked inside her soda bottle after slurping through the straw and said, "My *Guaraná* is all gone."

"So let's find the others and hit a couple of mild rides?"

With the whole group together again, they ended the night with the classic Ferris wheel and bumper car rides. But on the car rides, Vicky only went in the passenger seat. Leo had to explain to the others that, for some unknown reason, his sister had always been scared of driving. Probably her experience back in sixty-four did not do much to help her.

The park sound system was playing the radio hits of the time: "Rhythm Is a Dancer," "For Your Babies," "How Do You Do," "Decadence Avec Elegance," "Bed of Roses," and the megahit from the French baby singer Jordy, "Dur Dur D'être Bébé!"

"Guys, that's so neat! Are you listening to the music? These are the songs we listen to on the radio in nineteen ninety-three. Our favorite radio, Transamérica, plays them twenty-four seven."

Leo noticed that Vítor collected all sorts of plastic trash, theirs and anyone else's. From time to time, Vítor went to the machine and came back empty-handed. Leo couldn't help but wonder what that was all about and spoke with John. John did not need more than a few seconds to figure out what that was. However, he did not announce it to anyone. He just got close to Vítor and said, "Brilliant! Plastic!" Vítor smiled at him nonchalantly. Yes, it was plastic. John had just figured out what was the fuel of the time machine.

Soon it was ten o'clock, and the park was closing. They all grabbed one more soda and got ready to go.

"Did you like the trip, Joshua?"

"I did, Paul. A lot," he replied with his mouth covered in red, eating the last of his candy grapes.

Paul got the napkin that came with his soda, knelt close to the boy, and said, "Here, lil' lad, let's clean this mess up."

19 Rock'n'Roll To Axé Music In Thirty Years

Ten minutes past ten o'clock at night they were back to Rio Vermelho.

Vítor asked the time travelers, "Would you all like to go back home now?"

"But already!" Vicky whined.

Paul thought that was funny. "When are you going to think that it is not already?"

"Never. I wish you guys could stay forever. We're never going to see you again!"

"But, Vicky, enough is enough. It was sound meeting you folks and seeing the future. We had fun. But now it's time to go."

Paul could see in her eyes that she did not agree with it, and shook his head at her.

"What about you, Joshua? Will you go now?" Vítor asked.

"Yes, I want to go home, please. I really miss my parents."

"You kicking everyone out, Vítor!" Vicky protested again.

Vítor just ignored her this time.

Vicky realized she could not win and gave up. "Okay. I am sorry. After all, we did have fun. And that's thanks to your

machine. I guess I should be grateful for that."

Vítor shook his head and began setting up the machine.

"Well, I will set the machine for you first, okay, kiddo?" Vítor said to Joshua.

While the machine was being reset, Leo enjoyed the last few

minutes he had to chat with Ringo, as he had been doing since he joined the group.

Vicky took the chance to talk to Joshua.

"You enjoy the future?"

"There's a lot I don't get, but I did like it. I will miss you all. Please don't think you're the only one who will be sad."

"That's okay, Tiny. We'll all be okay."

"But you are about to cry."

"Don't start saying that. 'Cause I will really end up crying."

"All right, Joshua, you can come," Vítor called.

Joshua said good-bye, hugged everyone, and went into the machine. As he buckled up, he remembered, "The clothes! What do I do with the clothes?"

And Leo's idea was simple. "Tell your parents they were gifts from a foreigner."

Joshua replied to Leo with the okay sign he had learned from the 1993 children. Vítor closed the hatch and started the machine.

Vicky tried but could not hold back a tear that insisted on rolling down her face.

"Now I will send you guys home," Vítor said to George, Ringo, Paul, and John. "Is May first, nineteen sixty-four, okay?"

"We have the BBC interview." Paul remembered.

John asked, "Can you send us to the BBC radio in London?"

"That's okay, but I can only get you there by one a.m."

"One a.m.?"

"Yes, because of the time zone. It's a three-hour time zone difference."

"Your machine travels through years and centuries, but it can't travel hours?"

"What can I do? I'm not perfect." He then suggested, "Do you guys want to spend the night here and head back tomorrow morning? This way you'll be there just in time for the interview."

Vicky looked at Paul with a hopeful smile. He shook his head at her as if dismissing any ideas from her mind and told Vítor, "May first at one in the morning, is that right? Just leave us in

London. We have a place to stay."

"Okay. Wait just a few minutes."

"Careful not to bring someone we don't want back here," Ringo joked. "You won't have strong blokes like us to protect you anymore."

Vítor paid no attention to this talk and went into his machine. The others kept on making small talk. Vicky, however, did not say a word. She was holding back her tears as much as she could, but it was getting stronger than she.

Paul came near her. "You're not going to cry, right, girl?"

"Will you think of me when you're gone? I mean back in your time?"

"I will not forget you, Vitória."

She gave him a hug and started to cry.

Paul wiped her tears and whispered, "Hey, listen, I get the whole story of girls dreaming of getting married to their favorite stars. But I'm sure you will find someone special for you, even if it's not Vítor. Okay?"

She raised her eyebrows in disbelief, but nodded in agreement, which made Paul smile approvingly.

"Those two are so in love." John joked with George, and they both laughed.

Ringo and Leo said their final words to each other as well. As for Vítor, he had just finished setting up all the time coordinates.

"It's all set, guys. London, April twenty-ninth, nineteen sixty-four. It's now ten forty, so you'll get there at around one-fifty a.m. of May first. You'll land in some famous place in the city. Maybe Big Ben, something like that."

"Big Ben? Not fair!"

The guys laughed at the irony, said their good-byes to the children and went in the machine.

Vítor closed the hatch and turned the key that made the machine work.

And, at last, the four boys from Liverpool went back to '64. Vicky leaned against a pillar, looked at the moon, and let her mind travel there.

After a while in silence, Leo looked at Vítor and asked, "What are you going to do now?"

"I think … I will destroy this machine. It's already fulfilled its purpose. Keeping it is inviting trouble. Playing with time is pretty darn dangerous."

Leo looked at his sister and commented, "Yeah, I see how it was dangerous to you."

"What's the matter, momma's boy? You know we're over."

Leo laughed at him. "Then why does it bother you that I say it?"

"Because it bugs me to talk about it. Okay!"

"Yes, of course it bugs you. You are the only guy whose girlfriend cheated on with … yourself!"

"Leo."

Vítor's tone of voice was one of threat. So Leo preferred to hush. But he knew that Vítor just wished it was over. He just wished life was as easy as it was for grownups. They had it all figured out: beginning, middle, and end. And they always laughed at them when they got upset over girlfriend matters.

These thoughts were suddenly interrupted by a grownup's voice:

"Oh my! How long has it been I haven't seen this sad little face? Tell me, is that still because of Paul? It's been, like, thirty years!"

The voice had come from the gate, and the question had been directed to Vicky. The girl and the two boys looked toward the gate. They saw a fifty-something-year-old man wearing jeans and a button-up shirt. He seemed to be in a very good mood.

Vicky asked, feeling a little lost, "Who are you?"

The man replied, "My name is Leonardo Ferreira. I have been a singer and composer of Bahian and Northeastern music for the past ten years. But that is not the name or the music you know me by."

"Come again?"

He looked into her eyes and repeated a line that made her understand, "You are odd, eh!"

Vicky smiled in disbelief and asked, "Johnny?"

The man took off his glasses and laughed. "Of course it's me! Have I changed so much in thirteen years?"

Vicky ran to hug him while Vítor and Leo looked at each other, clueless.

"I never thought I would see you again."

"Do you think I'd lose track of you after what you did for me that day?"

Vítor decided to ask, "What is going on here? Didn't John Lennon die thirteen years ago?"

John explained, "True. John Lennon did die, thirteen years ago. And I would still be dead today if a girl, who was actually just born at the time, hadn't alerted me to it."

Vítor looked at Vicky, not knowing how to react. "Vicky, you—"

John went on, "Vicky went to 1980 a few days before I was supposed to be ... you know, and told me everything. She showed me newspapers from the day after."

"Then you escaped?"

"Not officially. Remember that stupid historical continuum and how we should not alter it, blah blah blah? I figured that was right. So I found a way to let John Lennon die on that day. But I changed things a little so no one would know I had actually survived."

"How's that?" Vicky did not get it.

"Well, if you grab a newspaper that talks about it, you'll see that it's a little bit different than what you think you know."

"And that's why you must not alter history. Now we don't know what we know anymore."

"Vítor! Is that how your mother raised you?" And he looked back at Vicky. "Thank you, girl. You saved my life."

"*Oxe*, you're welcome! Thank you for taking me seriously. So where have you been?"

"I moved to Brazil. I love this place. I have been living in Salvador, keeping an eye on all the mischief you've been up to for the past thirteen years."

"And singing *Axé* music?"

"Watch the way you talk, kiddo. There is plenty of good music in Bahia and in the Northeast. Including mine."

"Which ones are yours?"

"A lot of stuff famous people sing is mine. Darn it! If you can't recognize my music, what kind of a Beatles fan are you?"

"How could I? I thought you were dead. Besides, I don't listen to *Axé* music."

"Watch the way you refer to it, I said! People use the phrase *Axé* music to include all sorts of crappy stuff. Maybe now you'll listen to your land's music a bit more."

Vítor, Vicky, and Leo were perplexed by the story. Leo could not help but ask, "John Lennon! This is insane! Does Yoko Ono know you're alive?"

John got upset. "I wanted her to. But I thought that it would not be safe to let her know."

"What?"

"And Paul? Have you seen him?" Vicky asked, excited.

"I knew you'd ask that. That's why I came here today. We wrote down your address. When we went back to sixty-four, we made a pledge that we would get back here at this same date and time and surprise you."

"But ... only you are here. Where is everyone else? Humph! Paul forgot about me, didn't he?"

"Nah, it was probably because of what happened to me. I don't think Paul forgot about you because he is on a tour in Brazil." And looking in her eyes, he revealed, "I came to pick you up to go see him." John showed Vicky two tickets to Paul McCartney's concert in São Paulo.

"John Lennon! Paul is in São Paulo! My mom would never let me go to Sampa[12] with you!"

"I know. I know who your mother is. But that's why we have a time machine."

"What? Are you going to take advantage of my machine?"

"Is that how your mother raised you, Vítor?"

"He wants to destroy the machine," Leo reported.

"You still have that stupid idea, eh. Just forget about that, mate. Why would you want to destroy something you went through so much to build? You got all mad at Paul because he suggested you build a second one."

"No, he got all mad at Paul because he's jealous of him and Vicky," Leo teased.

John giggled. "Yeah, that too. But seriously. Instead of doing something that stupid, find a safe storage for it. This way, whenever you need it, it will be there for you."

Vítor was not sure what he would do anymore. He just sighed and said, "Listen, if you guys are traveling to Sampa, just do it, okay? Take the machine. Take whatever you want. It's got plenty of fuel. I am going to bed."

"Leo, do you mind staying behind?" she asked her brother, unsure of how he felt to be left aside.

---

12 Nickname for the city of São Paulo.

"Not really. I'm going home. I am not Paul McCartney's fan. If at least Ringo was here... Besides, Mom doesn't know I am with you guys. She's going to yell at me for getting home so late."

"Oh, by the way," Vítor said to Vicky, "my mom is telling yours everything we did. Get ready."

Vicky swallowed. Not only was she still single, she was also going to spend the rest of her life under house arrest. That was not fair. Well, there were only a few more hours left in the day— maybe her final hours of freedom. Not wasting any more time, she headed to Sampa with John. At least she would get to see Paul one more time.

20 *In Time For The Concert*

In São Paulo, Vicky and John got to the Pacaembu Stadium, the place where Paul McCartney was holding his concert. Toward the end of the concert, however, they could not resist trying to go meet him. It was time for some action. They sneaked around most of security and entered the backstage area, trying to find Paul's dressing room without being spotted. However, less than a hundred feet away, they were found.

"Hey! You there! You're not allowed here!" a security guard yelled.

"Oh, brother," Vicky whined.

"Get those two over there!"

It was as if the whole São Paulo police force was after them.

"Legs, what are you good for!" said Vicky. John was used to Brazilian phrases by now. He knew that idiom meant *run!*

And running and hiding and weaving between one, two, three officers they went, until Vicky saw Paul and his wife Linda heading to their dressing room.

"Paul!" she shouted, sliding on the floor, trying to keep her balance.

Paul looked, but did not see anyone. He and Linda looked at each other. They were almost sure someone had called. But no one was there. They looked again and walked into the dressing room.

Vicky and John had had to hide from another security person. And Vicky seemed to do it so well that John asked, "Girl, have you done this before?"

"Not in a concert, no. But at my new school I had to run away from hall monitors. They spotted me wearing a bracelet in the playground. And we're not allowed to wear jewelry. Anyway, I was caught."

"Oh. I hope that does not mean we will get caught. That will be it. We'll get kicked out."

"Probably not. I did give them a run for their money. I only got caught because one of the monitors sneaked behind a pillar while I was running. And he was huge. Like, huge!" Vicky said that and noticed the way had cleared. "There. Now. It's clear. Let's go."

Vicky and John outwitted the security guards for a few seconds. Slowly tiptoeing, they reached the door to the dressing room, which was shut. Carefully, she began to open it and was able to take a peek inside.

When they noticed the door opening, Paul and Linda looked that way.

But out there, more trouble was coming their way.

"There they are!"

Vicky got scared and tried to run, pulling John by the hand. But at that very moment, they were caught.

"No! Let me go!" she screamed. And, as the security guards dragged them away, she called out, "Paul!"

"We're his friends!" John said without anyone really paying attention to him. "Let us go talk to him!"

"Yes, that's right. And I am Cinderella."

"It's me! Vicky! Paul, help me! Paul!"

Paul heard that and remembered that evening, twenty-nine years before, when Vicky called for help, asking him to save her from Gilmar. Startled, he glanced at Linda and said, almost in a whisper, "Vicky?"

He left Linda trying to figure out what on earth he was talking about and zoomed out of the dressing room toward where he heard the cries coming from. He saw both Vicky and John but only recognized one of them. He spoke to the security guards, "Hey, you guys, hold it! Hold it! Let them go!"

No one really understood what or why, so they just froze the way they were. Paul looked at her and asked, "Vicky? Is that really you?"

She smiled and nodded.

"Come give me a hug, girl!"

The security guys let them go. She ran toward Paul, and John walked to them.

Paul saw John and actually thought he knew him.

The head of security promptly tried to apologize. "Mr. Paul, we had no idea."

"No, it's okay," he said, moving away from Vicky. "She's just an old friend of mine. Now could you leave us alone, please?"

With this request, Paul let the security crew go.

Linda arrived at the door at this moment. Paul looked back at John as if trying to figure out who he was.

"Paul, you don't remember your good old friend anymore?"

Paul could not believe the idea that crossed his mind. He looked at Vicky, inquisitive, taken aback by the prospect of who that could be.

She clarified, "I spent some time with John in November nineteen eighty."

Paul turned to him, perplexed, as any other person who had lived through that experience would be. He stared at John, still not able to believe what he saw. Shy tears began to fall from his eyes, and neither friend could say a word. They simply exchanged a tight hug, as if they had not seen each other in many years.

"Why have you never told me anything, my friend?"

"I couldn't, Paul. I could not let anyone know."

"What exactly is going on here?" Linda asked, still lost.

"Linda, this is Vicky," Paul began to explain while subtly wiping his eyes. "Remember I used to tell you about her?"

Linda looked at the girl and said, "Vicky?" Then she shook her head at Paul in disbelief.

He nodded at her reassuringly.

"Paul! I … So you're *the* Vicky? The time-travel girl?"

Again, she smiled and nodded.

Well, it *was* 1993. The girl was about thirteen, curly hair…

Heck, she was even wearing the same clothes. Linda could have sworn that the little teenager had just gotten home from going crazy on a shopping spree in New York City in the late seventies or early eighties. And they *were* in Brazil after all. Could it be that the whole wacky story was true?

"Oh my! Paul used to talk a lot about you. At one point I really thought he was losing it."

"So now you believe me?" Paul teased his wife.

Vicky sighed, looked down, and said, "So you are Linda McCartney. I've always wanted to meet you. You're one lucky lady!"

Linda giggled, knowing exactly what Vicky meant since she knew the whole story by heart.

Then Paul suggested, "Let's go into our dressing room."

All four of them went in. Paul sat down and pulled a chair for Vicky. Then he joked, "Girl, you have not changed a bit in thirty years!"

"Really? That's too bad I can't say the same about you!"

"Hey! That's not a nice thing to say!"

Linda, who, like John, was still standing, couldn't take her eyes off him. She then risked a conclusion. "But if ... if you are Vicky, judging by what I have just heard, my only possible conclusion is that you are ..."

She stopped right there. She did not dare to go beyond imagination. But Paul confirmed, "John Lennon."

Linda's reaction was the same as anyone else's. "John Lennon? I-I ... don't ..." And again she stopped halfway through and laughed in disbelief.

Then Paul asked, "But where have you been all this time?"

"I have been in Brazil, making music and keeping an eye on this kiddo to make sure she'd behave."

"Not even Yoko knows he is alive!" Vicky reported.

"Not even Yoko?" Paul was shocked.

John shook his head. "I did not want to take the risk of being found."

"But, John! Now what! You're going to have to tell her. It is

144

just not fair. I don't care what you say, if you don't, I will."

"Paul, now *I* am really mad. You were doing a concert in Brazil and didn't come to see me. John said you guys had planned on coming. Why didn't you? Why didn't anyone?"

"Because John had the address! He didn't tell you that much, did he?"

"Not really," John replied, faking an innocent face.

"We did not know your last names or anything, y'know. How could we come looking for you? I did have backstage passes with your name though. I figured you'd be smart enough to try to get them."

"Hmm, maybe I would have … if I could *afford* to come to *São Paulo* for your concert. Besides, I am thirteen. Last time Leo and I went to a concert in *Salvador*, my mom did not fall asleep until we got home. At three in the morning! And Aunt Regina was with us, mind you."

"Her mom keeps her and her brother on a tight leash." John remarked.

"Yeah. And she always catches me when I try to go around her rules. Like when Leo and I skipped school to go to the mall, old man, we had the perfect plan. She found out. She found out! We got into a lot of trouble."

"Vicky, you're always looking for trouble," Paul laughed.

"Paul, I am not. I'm an angel who never does anything wrong."

"Sure you are. An angel whose specialty is to get herself in trouble … and convince grownups she ain't doing nothing wrong. Your words, not mine. Remember?"

"Uh, yeah, whatever. Thank goodness Vítor and I were smart enough to plan out the weekend as a study session. She still thinks we're studying for the finals."

"But finals are not till June."

"No, in Brazil school ends in December. Now, when Aunt Cláudia tells my mom what she found out, I'm as good as dead."

The grownups laughed at that remark, and John denied it, "Nah, you'll just be grounded for life. But you'll survive."

"You think we can talk Aunt Cláudia into not giving us away, John?"

"Not a chance," John said.

"Yeah, no," Vicky agreed, looking down.

"Vicky," Paul said, shaking his head, "what are the odds your mum will actually believe a wacky story like that? Chances are she'll think Cláudia has been smoking something."

Vicky chuckled at the thought of her mom picturing Aunt Cláudia smoking something and coming up with that story. Mom would never allow her to set foot at Vítor's house again.

"I sure hope you're right, Paul. But just in case I get grounded for life—or murdered—I'm glad I got to see you one last time."

"What do you mean one last time? I'm not losing track of you again. And … I guess I can try to make sure you don't get murdered by your own mother. At least that doesn't involve getting punched in the face."

"Well, I wouldn't count on that when it comes to my mom. But, hey, after all these years, you're still my hero!"